FLIGHT
TO THE HORIZON

By the Author

The Road to Wings

Flight to the Horizon

Visit us at www.boldstrokesbooks.com

FLIGHT
TO THE HORIZON

by

Julie Tizard

2020

FLIGHT TO THE HORIZON

ISBN 13: 978-1-63555-331-4

THIS TRADE PAPERBACK ORIGINAL IS PUBLISHED BY
BOLD STROKES BOOKS, INC.
P.O. BOX 249
VALLEY FALLS, NY 12185

FIRST EDITION: JANUARY 2020

CREDITS
EDITOR: SHELLEY THRASHER
PRODUCTION DESIGN: STACIA SEAMAN
TOP COVER PHOTO BY SUSAN RENEE
COVER DESIGN BY SHERI (HINDSIGHTGRAPHICS@GMAIL.COM)

Acknowledgments

I want to express my deep appreciation to everyone at Bold Strokes Books for your patience and support in the writing of this book. Thanks to my editor, Shelley Thrasher, for your excellent guidance. To one of my favorite authors, Justine Saracen, I appreciate your outstanding advice.

To my friend and fellow crew member, Flight Attendant Lisa Carroll, thank you for your expert technical advice. And to all the flight attendants it has been my honor to fly with, thank you for taking care of all of us. Special thanks to Lieutenant Commander Jude Litzenberger, US Navy (ret.), for your guidance on all things nautical. To my readers who have given me such great encouragement, you have my deepest gratitude.

Despite what you are about to read, flying really is the safest way to travel. Trust me.

For Sue. Thank you for my Happily Ever After.

Dedicated to my mother,
Barbara Lou Tiffany Tizard.

Your love of life, of laughter, and of adventure has inspired me.
You have always been the wind beneath my wings.

Prologue

Monday, April 28

"Trans Global 801, cleared for takeoff, runway two-five right."

"Roger, Trans Global 801, cleared for takeoff," the first officer said.

Captain Kerri Sullivan pushed both throttles forward slightly to turn the massive Boeing 767 onto the darkened runway. The centerline lights were hard to see with the thick fog and only a quarter mile of visibility. Before takeoff, as usual, Kerri mentally reviewed her abort procedures in case of an emergency. She took a deep breath to focus her mind and body and smoothly pushed both throttles up to takeoff power. "Check thrust."

"Thrust set," the first officer said. Kerri pushed forward slightly on the yoke to keep the nose wheel on the centerline. She glanced at the two columns of engine instruments—all in the green. Excitement tingled through her as the giant engines increased to full power. No matter how many times she did this, the deep growl of the engines always thrilled her, as did the low vibration moving up from her feet through her chest as she accelerated down the runway.

"One hundred knots." *I'm in the high-speed regime now.* The nose wheel steering became more sensitive as the plane quickly accelerated. The air noise increased, and she glanced at the engine instruments one more time—all good.

"V-one." The first officer called out the go/no-go speed. Kerri moved her right hand from the throttles to the yoke, indicating she was now committed to the takeoff. Suddenly, the nose of the jet abruptly swerved to the right.

"Engine fail!" the first officer shouted. Kerri instinctively stepped on the left rudder pedal to bring the airplane back to the centerline. She slammed both throttles forward against the stop. "Rotate," he called out.

No, not yet. Fly the jet, fly the jet. Stabilize it on the runway before you get into the air.

Kerri kept her left leg fully extended on the rudder pedal to counteract the yaw from the failed engine. In the dark fog, the dim centerline lights changed colors from white to red. *I have only two thousand feet of runway left.* Gently pulling back on the big yoke, she coaxed the crippled jet into the air. Only grayness lay in front of her. She looked down to the electronic attitude indicator and pulled the nose up to ten degrees of pitch. The aircraft, at maximum takeoff weight of three hundred and twenty thousand pounds, barely crept up into the air. *Come on, baby. Climb for me.*

After what felt like forever, she was finally one hundred feet above the ground. "Positive rate of climb. Gear up." The first officer raised the wheel-shaped landing gear lever. Without the drag from the wheels, the jet climbed a tiny bit faster. Kerri looked at the altimeter—almost four hundred feet above the ground. "Pull for runway heading." She would continue straight ahead over the shoreline into the dark night.

Her left leg shook from holding the rudder pedal full against the stop. She was climbing at only two hundred feet per minute, with the jet somewhat stabilized. Kerri brought her right hand down to the center console and felt for the unique shape of the rudder trim knob. Turning the knob to the left, she held it until the pressure on her left leg decreased. The altimeter read eight hundred feet above the ground. "Set clean maneuver speed." The first officer rotated the airspeed knob to two hundred thirty knots. "Autopilot one is coming on," Kerri announced.

With the autopilot helping her control the plane, she focused on analyzing what had happened. "What have we got?"

"We lost all oil quantity from the right engine," the first officer said.

"Any indication of fire?"

"No."

"Okay. No chance for a restart. Run the engine-shutdown checklist." The airplane slowly accelerated. "Flaps up."

Kerri focused like a laser beam as she reviewed the multiple tasks before her. She had to fly the jet and keep it stabilized, monitor the copilot while he ran the checklist, and make a plan to get this jet safely on the ground with only one engine. The weather was crappy back at Los Angeles, but it was no better at any other airport for several hundred miles. She had to try to land back at LA. Continuously, she mentally reprioritized all these tasks. Adrenaline raced through her, but she stayed calm and in control. She didn't have time for fear. Her life, and the lives of her passengers and crew, depended on her.

"Tower, Trans Global 801 is declaring an emergency. We've lost an engine, and I need vectors back to LA for an instrument approach. Two hundred fifty-five souls on board."

"Trans Global 801, copy your emergency. Turn left heading one-six-zero. Contact SoCal Approach on one-three-five-point-one-five. Emergency equipment will be standing by."

"Trans Global 801, heading one-six-zero." Kerri picked up the flight interphone and rang the cabin call button. She briefed the flight attendants on what was going on, made an announcement to the passengers, then called the company dispatch.

The fog in LA had improved slightly to one-half-mile visibility. Good enough to land, but just barely. "Bob, I'm going to fly the ILS precision approach to runway two-five left. This will be right to minimums, so I need you to back me up."

Kerri briefed the approach, set up the navigation equipment, and mentally reviewed the single-engine approach procedures. She'd informed everyone she needed to and completed all the checklists. Now she just had to land this beast. She took another deep breath. Landing the plane with only one engine in a dark, foggy night would be her last, and most difficult, task. She had absolutely no room for error.

"Trans Global 801 emergency, turn left heading two-eight-zero, maintain two thousand feet until established on the localizer, cleared for the ILS approach runway two-five left."

"Trans Global 801 emergency, cleared for the approach," the copilot said.

Kerri slowly pulled back the throttle on her one remaining engine. "Speed one-ninety, flaps to ten." She kept her eyes glued to her attitude indicator and the flight-director bars. "Localizer capture," she called as she turned the jet onto the final approach course. "Glide slope is alive. Gear down, flaps to twenty, set final approach speed."

Kerri could no longer use the autopilot to help her fly the jet. As she descended into the darkness, she clicked the autopilot off. She would hand-fly this plane to a single-engine landing with only her skill and years of experience to count on. *Small corrections, small corrections. Stay on the glide slope. Watch your airspeed.*

She kept the flight director bars centered on the attitude indicator. "Approaching minimums," the first officer said. *I'm three hundred feet above the ground. No runway lights yet.*

"Decision height."

Kerri looked up from the instruments and saw faint strobe lights leading her to the runway threshold. "I have it. Landing." The computer voice said, "Fifty, forty, thirty, twenty, ten." She smoothly retarded the single throttle to idle and pulled back on the yoke to flare the jet. As the main wheels gently touched the runway, she flew the nose wheel down, lifted up on the thrust reverser lever, and stepped on the wheel brakes to stop the jet.

"Well, you both get to keep your jobs." The check pilot who'd been sitting behind them for the last two days made it sound like he was giving them a present. "Good job on your crew coordination and your briefings. Excellent approach, Captain. See you both back here at the training center in nine months." He turned the lights on in the cockpit, and the flight simulator settled back down onto the hydraulic actuators.

Kerri shook her copilot's hand as they left the sim. "Great job, Bob. Thanks for your help."

"Any time, Kerri. You fly a great airplane."

Riding the bus from the flight training center to the airport, Kerri had to make a conscious effort to breathe deeply and calm her heart rate. After two days of "dial-a-disaster" in the simulator, which tested her flying skills to the max, she'd cheated death multiple times and passed every emergency thrown at her.

I hate playing "You bet your job." I need a drink.

CHAPTER ONE

Thursday, May 1

Captain Kerri Sullivan put on her round hat with the gold trim on the bill, then walked down the exterior Jetway stairs to complete the walk-around inspection of her Boeing 767. She wasn't required to. Normally the first officer did it, but she liked to personally inspect her jet, as long as the weather was nice. When it rained or snowed, she exercised her "captain's privilege" and let the copilot take over. She'd paid enough dues during her flying career as an air force pilot, a copilot, and a 737 captain to earn this right. She chose to do the exterior inspection today because it was a beautiful day in Los Angeles, she was on her way to Maui, Hawaii, and because she loved looking at the magnificent aircraft she commanded.

Kerri loved everything about this jet. It was big, powerful, and fast. She had to admit that she was a bit of a size queen when it came to airplanes. The bigger it was, the more she enjoyed flying it. She waved to the aircraft mechanic, Smitty, as he did his own inspection.

"Hey, Smitty. How's she look today?" He'd been working on jets a lot longer than she'd been flying them.

"She's a beauty, Skipper." He always called her "Skipper," since he was a former navy aircraft mechanic. She appreciated the sacred bond between pilots and mechanics like Smitty. If he said her jet was safe to fly, she'd bet her life on his word.

These jets were thoroughly scrutinized because she would be flying over two thousand miles of open ocean to reach Hawaii. Maintenance made sure everything was perfect, and she always double-checked everything on the plane as well.

She knew every inch of this enormous aircraft and inspected each primary, secondary, and alternate pilot tube, static port, and angle of attack sensor. The flight control surfaces were the size of barn doors, and all ten of the big tires looked new and shiny. She paid special attention to the two massive engines. This aircraft was certified to fly on only one engine for up to three hours, but she'd never had to test that claim and wasn't about to on this flight. The huge engine intakes, giant fan blades, and thrust reversers were all in excellent condition. She stepped carefully around the baggage belt loaders, cargo lifts, and the fuel truck. A small army of people worked simultaneously to get the flight ready—aircraft mechanics, baggage loaders, caterers, fuelers, gate agents, flight attendants, and pilots. It was an amazing orchestration of skill and detail to get a plane with two hundred and fifty-five people ready to fly across the ocean. Kerri never failed to be impressed with the whole airline operation and beamed with pride to fly as a captain for Trans Global Airlines.

After she finished her inspection and returned to the Jetway stairs, the crew bus pulled up, and the six flight attendants got out with their black suitcases. She recognized Chief Purser George Cato and a few of the female flight attendants. A new woman in the group, a tall blonde, was strikingly beautiful. Butterflies fluttered in Kerri's stomach as she watched the newcomer ascend the stairs in her slightly snug blue uniform dress and black high heels.

When Kerri returned to the flight deck, her copilot, Joe Henderson, was already in the right seat doing his preflight setup. He was fairly new on the 767, and Kerri had flown with him before. He knew the standard operating procedures, was pleasant to work with, and his landings were coming along. Kerri had already decided that she would fly the leg to Maui and Joe would fly the return trip to LA. The airport in Maui, located in a valley between two mountains, had a short runway and wicked crosswinds. The difficult and dicey approach left no room for error, so she always did the landing in Maui. She let the copilots fly the approaches into Honolulu and Kona because they had long runways and no steep-terrain issues, but Maui was a different animal, so she took no chances there.

Kerri picked up the public-address handset. "All flight attendants, please come forward for the flight briefing." She took her flight plan and stood at the front of the jet waiting for them. "Hi, everyone. I'm Kerri, Joe is the first officer, and we have a beautiful day for flying. We will encounter some turbulence on the departure, so please stay in your jump seats, and I will call you when it's safe to get up. Our flying time is five hours and fifty-five minutes today. It should be smooth once we get over the ocean, and everything mechanical on the jet is good. Oh, and I'm an FFDO."

"So you're packing today, Captain?" George asked.

Kerri looked at her chief purser and shook her head as he snickered.

"Yes, I'm a federal flight deck officer, and I'm carrying a firearm today."

George amused Kerri every time he told the flight attendants she was "packing."

She continued. "If there's anything I can help you with, please let me know. Let's all have a great flight today."

❖

Flight Attendant Janine Case returned to her station in the mid-cabin and continued her preflight duties. She checked all the emergency equipment on board, the oxygen bottles, the slide rafts in the cabin doors, and then she inspected the food and beverage carts in the galley. Most people thought of flight attendants as glorified waitresses, but she took her job very seriously. She was responsible for the safety of her passengers, and if they had to do an emergency evacuation, she was in charge of getting the people off the airplane.

What was Captain Kerri Sullivan really like? She'd flown with women pilots before, but not many female captains. Even though women had been flying as airline pilots for several years, very few were 767 captains. She was certainly attractive—tall and athletic-looking, with short brown hair, a strong jaw, and expressive hands. Janine mainly noticed her warm brown eyes and ready smile. She oozed confidence, and many men probably found her intimidating. She hoped Kerri wasn't like many of the cocky, arrogant male captains.

Regardless of who the captain was, Janine was here to take care of her passengers and give them a nice flight experience to Hawaii. For many of them, a Hawaiian vacation was a lifetime dream come true. She hadn't been flying to the islands for very long, and she missed being at home, but she did enjoy the nice, long layovers on Hawaii's gorgeous beaches. She didn't socialize with the other flight attendants much, mainly because they often asked too many personal questions, but she did like to explore on her own and was looking forward to discovering Maui.

The chief purser, George, walked into the mid-cabin galley. "Hi, Janine. Need any help with anything, honey?"

"No. I'm good, but thanks for the offer."

"I have a few fresh flowers left, so I'm going to decorate the mid-cabin lavatories a bit. Would you like a red hibiscus for your hair? It'd look fabulous on you."

"Sure. Why not? Thanks, George."

He delicately placed the blossom behind her right ear. "You look absolutely gorgeous, Janine."

She was uncomfortable at the compliment and turned back to busying herself in the galley.

She checked the mid-cabin lavs once more before the

passengers started boarding, surprised at how beautiful George had made these common-looking restrooms. He'd whipped together tasteful floral arrangements on the stainless-steel countertops and made them look quite elegant. George Cato was famous in LA for going over and above his duties to give the passengers five-star service. He remembered the names of all the first-class passengers and how they liked their drinks. He always looked impeccable in his uniform and was the epitome of class and taste. She could learn a lot from him.

The passengers started boarding, and she helped people find their seats and stow their luggage. Soon the captain's voice sounded over the PA system.

"Good afternoon, ladies and gentlemen. This is Captain Kerri Sullivan, and I'd like to welcome you aboard Trans Global flight 501, Boeing 767 service to Maui. Our flight today will be five hours and fifty-five minutes, at a cruising altitude of thirty-six thousand feet. Current weather in Maui is perfect, as always. They are reporting a temperature of seventy-five degrees, light winds, and a few scattered clouds. We have a great day over the ocean, and on behalf of myself and all the employees of Trans Global, I invite you to sit back, relax, and enjoy the friendly skies." The captain sounded confident and professional, with a little mirth in her announcement, like she was happy to be flying. It was a nice change from some of the grumpy captains Janine had flown with. She liked the sound of Kerri's voice.

❖

Kerri was busy programming the flight computers, checking the fuel load, reviewing the departure procedure, and testing the radios. She was thorough and methodical in her preflight preparations, even though she'd done them more than a thousand times. She double-checked her first officer's takeoff data, and she expected him to review her work. Catching each other's errors, no matter how minor, was vital to working together as a crew.

As she moved her hands swiftly over the massive array of buttons, knobs, and dials, she had a brief flashback to the first Cessna 150 she'd learned to fly sixteen years ago. Smiling, she remembered her incredible journey to get to where she was today as a Boeing 767 captain.

"Here's your hot tea with two sugars, Captain."

"Thanks, George. How can you remember what everyone likes to drink? You're amazing."

"Well, I don't remember everyone I fly with. But I certainly remember the good captains like you, Kerri."

"Aw, thanks, George. I really like flying with you too." She was always delighted to see his name on her crew manifest.

"Here are your water bottles. Let me know if you need anything else." He handed each pilot a big plastic bottle with their name written on each one in beautiful calligraphy.

People interrupted her at least a dozen times, asking her questions, before they shut the cabin door for push back. These interruptions never flustered her or made her impatient. She simply stayed focused on her job and prided herself on treating all her coworkers with courtesy and respect. She glanced down at her crew manifest at the new name, Janine Case. *What's your story, Janine?*

"Captain, we've got everyone on board and are ready to close up. Do you need anything else?" the gate agent asked.

"No, thank you. We're all set."

Kerri briefed her first officer on their oceanic clearance, the taxi route, the departure she would be flying, and the emergency procedures.

"Any questions, Joe?"

"No. I'm good."

"Then let's run the preflight checklist." They were on their way to Hawaii, and a tingle of excitement raced through Kerri. *I love my job!*

CHAPTER TWO

"Trans Global 501, cleared for takeoff, runway two-five right."

"Roger, Trans Global 501, cleared for takeoff, two-five right," Joe answered.

Kerri flipped on the exterior light switches and taxied the 767 onto the runway, slowly turning the small tiller wheel to control the nose wheel. The nose wheels were actually twenty feet behind the cockpit, so she had to make her body go past the runway centerline first, then turn to get lined up. This jet was so big she couldn't even see the wingtips or the engines from the cockpit windows, so she used reference points in the flight deck to know where the wheels and engines were. She still felt like this jet was strapped to her body, just like she'd learned when she was an air force pilot, but now she felt like she was flying a giant building rather than a hot, fast fighter.

In many ways, piloting something this large was much more difficult than handling a smaller plane because the margin for error was so small. The Boeing 767 was an amazingly sophisticated machine with over a million parts and miles of wiring. Kerri found flying this jet endlessly challenging.

She pushed the throttles up to takeoff thrust, felt the low rumble of the engines coming up to full power, checked her engine instruments, and steered with her feet as she accelerated down the runway. "V-one. Rotate," Joe called. Kerri gently pulled back on the yoke as the mighty aircraft gracefully rose into the air. A giant smile stretched across her face. Flying was nothing short of magic.

They received clearance to their coast-out fix and climbed to the cruise altitude. It was a beautiful day with blue skies, some high, thin, wispy clouds, and a smooth ride. Kerri looked down at the big ships in Long Beach harbor. From her vantage, they resembled toys in a bathtub. She thought of her dad when he was a ship captain in the merchant marine. The sun shone in front of them, slightly low on the horizon. She put on her Ray-Ban sunglasses and enjoyed the view from the best seat in the house.

Kerri loved looking at the ocean with the sun sparkling on it like a field of diamonds slowly undulating on the water's surface. Few people got to see the lines in the ocean from the wakes of the big cargo ships. These liquid trails remained visible for hours and reminded her of the contrails jets made in the sky at high altitude. A radio call interrupted her sightseeing.

"Trans Global 501, Los Angeles Center, change to enroute advisory frequency. Aloha."

"Trans Global 501, changing to enroute frequency. See you on the flip side, Center," Joe replied.

Kerri leveled off at thirty-six thousand feet, turned on the autopilot, and ran the cruise checklist. She looked at all three altimeters, ranked the inertial reference navigation computers, and tested the long-range, high-frequency radios. All the mechanical systems were critical to helping her safely cross the ocean, and she verified that everything was exactly as it was supposed to be before they traveled too far from land. Kerri watched the first officer record their flight data on the paper flight plan. Even though they were flying a modern electronic jet with advanced navigation equipment, they still backed up their position reporting with a paper flight plan and an air navigation chart, just in case a problem occurred over the vast expanse of water.

She was out of the busy LA airspace, with its annoying radio chatter and aircraft traffic, and the sky beckoned her. The sunlight cast soft shades of gold and pink on the cirrus clouds above her, and the scattered cumulus clouds beneath her looked like white popcorn floating over the deep-blue sea. She especially loved watching the horizon, where the sea and the sky embraced each other endlessly. They were always next to each other, separated by a thin line, but never really apart.

A twinge of melancholy pierced her happiness. She wanted someone to share this with. A woman who understood her love of flying, who wanted to travel with her, a loving woman to come home to and to shower her love upon. It was the only thing missing from her otherwise great life, but it was a huge missing piece. She would never reach the horizon, but would she ever find the love of her life?

❖

Janine heard the ding and saw the Fasten Seat Belt signs come on. She felt the airplane shake, held on to the galley cart, and heard Kerri's voice over the PA.

"This is Captain Sullivan. We're going through an area of turbulence and I've turned on the Fasten Seat Belt sign. Flight attendants, please take your jump seats."

George and Janine strapped themselves into their jump seats.

"I love that Kerri always looks out for us," George said.

"She does?"

"Oh, yes. She backed me up during a confrontation with a passenger and she's stood up for us with maintenance too."

Janine appreciated a captain who tried to be considerate. She'd flown with so many male captains who talked down to flight attendants, like they were lesser human beings. A few male captains were downright rude to her. She'd also encountered the ones who hit on anything in a skirt, like cavemen who thought flight attendants were there for their own personal amusement. She'd crossed paths with a couple of male pilots who refused to take "No" for an answer. One guy had even stalked her, and she'd had to report him to the company. They just transferred him to another base.

She'd flown out of LA for only a few months, but she got the scoop on the problem pilots from the "stew underground." Fortunately, out of eight hundred pilots in LA, only a handful were real jerks, and everyone knew who they were. These guys got off on abusing their positions of power over other crewmembers, and she avoided them. When they had a captain who really supported them, communicated with them, and understood their jobs, the flight went so much better. Kerri Sullivan seemed like a good captain.

After the turbulence, she'd completed her first service, and the passengers were quietly reading, playing video games, or watching movies. With a few moments to herself, she sat in her jump seat and looked at her flight schedule. They would land at six p.m. Hawaii time, then depart the next evening at ten p.m. She had twenty-seven hours to explore Maui and wondered what she'd find. She'd heard a few of the other flight attendants talk about going to get Maui tacos for dinner, and one woman said she enjoyed renting a bike at the hotel. These were nice, long relaxing layovers and a welcome break from issues back at home she didn't want to deal with. She gazed out the small window in the aft door at the blue sky with pink clouds. What did Captain Sullivan, uh, Kerri, like to do on her long layovers?

❖

After two hours of flight, Kerri rang the cabin call button. "Hey, George. Can we get set up for a restroom break?"

"Yes, Captain. I'll be right there."

George arrived at the flight deck to allow Joe to step back to use the lavatory. "How's everything going, Kerri?"

"Good. We'll be about fifteen minutes early and should have a smooth ride for the rest of the flight. How's Doctor Michael?"

"Oh, about the same. Thanks for asking. He has good days and bad, but he generally remembers who I am."

"Are you working the return flight tonight?"

"Yes. That way I'm only away from home fifteen hours. Our niece spends the night at the house, and I'm home before Michael wakes up. We have breakfast together, and then I go to bed."

"I don't know how you do that, George. I'd be a zombie on that all-night return leg."

"I'm used to it, and it works for Michael and me. After forty years together, I need to be with him as much as I can."

"I get it. Doctor Michael is a very lucky man."

"Oh, Kerri, I'm the lucky one. He's still my dreamboat after all these years." George's voice caught as he spoke those last words.

Kerri changed the subject. "What's the story on the new flight attendant, Janine?"

"Oh, you noticed her, did you?" He laughed with his deep, baritone voice. "Well, she's fairly new to LA. Transferred here from Chicago a few months ago. No one knows much about her, and she kind of sticks to herself on the layovers. She's pleasant and very professional, but some people refer to her as the Ice Queen. I like her, though. What do you think of her?"

"I think I want to invite her to join all of us at the hotel pool bar. Maybe get to know her a little bit." Heat rose up Kerri's neck.

"Uh-huh, I bet you do, Kerri. Well, good luck with that." He laughed at her as he let Joe back into the cockpit and returned to the cabin.

❖

Kerri's voice sounded over the PA. "Ladies and gentlemen, this is Captain Sullivan again. Our flight attendants will be handing out the cards for our Halfway to Hawaii game for all you aspiring navigators out there. In a few minutes, I'll give you our takeoff time, the distance in miles of our flight, our true airspeed, and the average wind component for this flight. Your job is to calculate, to the nearest hour, minute, and second, the exact time we will cross the midpoint of this flight to Hawaii. The person who gets closest to the actual crossing time will win a prize. Good luck and have fun."

Janine heard that mirth in Kerri's voice again. She clearly loved doing stuff like this silly game with the passengers.

She and the other flight attendants handed out the game cards while some passengers came up with calculators. *Who brings a calculator on a trip to Hawaii?* Some passengers took this game very seriously as they worked hard on the navigation math problem. After Kerri gave them the information, many of the passengers handed her back their game cards covered with calculations, while some people just made a wild guess.

Janine carried all the cards up to the front of the plane. "Here are the game cards, George."

"Why don't you take them to the cockpit, Janine. I'm about to start my dessert service."

"Okay." Janine rang the cockpit.

After Joe let her in, she stood quietly just inside the cockpit door, looking at all the instruments and lights. The flight deck was so complicated. *How do they remember what all this stuff does?*

The view out the big windows was spectacular, and she bent down for a better look. The expanse of dark blue water around them was endless, and the sun near the horizon made the sky glow with golden light.

"Hi, Janine. How's everything going?" Kerri asked.

"Here are the game cards." She handed Kerri the stack of them.

"Thanks. You sorted them for us?"

"I just arranged them in order of their time estimate. I hope that's okay."

"Sure. It saves me from having to do that. Have a seat." She pointed to the fold-down jump seat behind the captain's seat.

Janine sat down and looked around while Kerri sorted through the cards. Black button circuit breakers covered the back wall of the flight deck from floor to ceiling. The roof had more circuit breakers, plus columns of switches and lights labeled Fuel, Hydraulics, Pressurization, Ice/Rain, Electrical, Fire, Air Conditioning, and Lights. It was a dizzying array. The forward instrument panel had six big electronic screens and smaller dials, with a center console between the pilots filled with radios, more screens, keyboards, and the two big engine throttles. Radio calls came over the cockpit speakers, with pilots of other aircraft rattling off their positions over the ocean. The cockpit intimidated and fascinated her. *What kind of mind does it take to fly this?* She wanted to ask Kerri what each button and light was for.

Janine watched Kerri's hands as she sorted through the game cards. Her fingers were long, her hands tan and strong, with prominent veins on the back and pale-pink nail polish on short nails. She looked at the back of Kerri's head as she worked. Her neck was slender under her short, dark-brown hair. Janine admired broad, muscular shoulders under her white uniform shirt, with four gold captain's stripes on each epaulet. She looked up, and Kerri was staring at her. *Busted.*

"Here you go, Janine. The person in twenty-five C won, eight E was second closest, and fifteen A was third."

"Thanks." Janine suddenly felt nervous and left the flight deck.

❖

After Janine left abruptly, her perfume lingered in the air. Kerri recognized the scent—Aromatics, by Clinique. Very few women could pull off wearing this perfume. It was spicy, with a bit of musk. It could be overpowering on some women, but it seemed to fit Janine. Kerri didn't memorize perfume scents, but this one was special, and she remembered it from a lover who'd worn it several years ago.

That lover had been beautiful, like Janine, but she'd been a liar and a cheat, and their affair didn't last long. The best thing about her had been that perfume. That woman was one in a long string of lovers and failed relationships. Kerri had always been attracted to beautiful women, but she'd never been able to figure out how to make a hot attraction turn into a real relationship.

Some of the women she'd dated were looking for a sugar mama who would support them in luxury. Others were used to being admired for their beauty but didn't have anything else to offer, such as the ability to carry on a conversation. Still others were impressed by what Kerri did for a living and used her as a trophy. Most of the women she'd been involved with were pretty but vapid, or completely self-centered.

After her last ugly breakup, which cost her a great deal of money and angst, she decided to take a break from women altogether for a while. She'd spent a lot of time trying to figure out what was really important to her in a life partner. After much soul-searching, and several months of therapy, she finally realized she wanted a woman who accepted her as she was, and who was sincere and honest. Kerri had changed her perspective. She was through wasting her time with women who were only flashy and hot. She longed to meet a lady who was attractive but also kind and loving. And, of course, great in bed. That was a must. *Where is all this coming from?* It was Janine's perfume—a sense memory filled with possibility.

Janine was certainly beautiful. She was a tall, Nordic blonde with ice-blue eyes, full lips, and luscious curves. She was also clearly intelligent and articulate. Kerri had dated a flight attendant once before. When it hadn't worked out, their situation at work had become very awkward because this woman carried a grudge. She'd trashed Kerri with the other flight attendants, and it'd taken a long time to make things right on the job. After that, Kerri vowed to never mix work and women again. Janine might be gorgeous, but even if she did like other women, she was off-limits.

CHAPTER THREE

Janine checked her watch. They would be starting their descent into Maui in about an hour, so she handed out the Hawaii agriculture forms to the passengers. Hawaii was very strict about protecting their islands from non-native invasive species and checked all incoming bags and cargo. Janine referred to them as the Fruit Police. She walked up to the front of the cabin. "George, do the pilots need Hawaiian agricultural forms?"

"Yes, they do. Could you please take them to the cockpit?"

"Sure." She rang the cockpit. "I have your agriculture forms. You guys need a restroom break before we start down?"

"Yes, Janine."

Joe let her into the flight deck, and then he stepped out.

"Do you have any plans for your layover?" Kerri asked.

"Not really. I've never been to Maui before. I just want to explore a little."

"You'll love it. It's just so beautiful. We all usually meet at the hotel pool bar after we check in. First round's on me. I hope you'll join us."

"Thanks. I might. What do you like to do on your layovers?"

"Just walk along the beach or do some paddleboarding. The hotel where we stay is great. Lots to do there."

Janine didn't generally like to drink with the other crew members. She'd seen a few too many pilots drink too much, then get very flirtatious and handsy, but she might make an exception tonight.

After returning to the cabin to complete her before landing duties, butterflies stirred in Janine's stomach, as they always did before each landing. The sound of the landing gear coming down and the rumble of the big wheels locking into position under the aircraft gave her a thrill unique to flying. Looking at her passengers as they descended into Maui, she saw exhilaration, excitement, and even joy on their faces. They were all ready for a fabulous vacation, and she could hardly wait to see what this new adventure would bring.

George had told her to expect a bumpy arrival because of the mountains and gusty winds at the airport. He'd also warned her to buckle in tight to her jump seat because the plane often made a very firm landing on the short runway. Janine was braced for a hard touchdown but was surprised when she felt a very smooth landing, followed by the roar of the engines in reverse thrust and rapid deceleration of the plane. *Impressive, Captain Kerri.*

After all the passengers deplaned and they cleared customs, the crew piled into the van and rode through the Maui countryside to their hotel. Janine was thrilled when she saw the beautiful grounds, tennis courts, and luau area. *This is such a gorgeous place.*

"Let's all meet down at the main pool bar in fifteen minutes," Kerri said.

Janine entered her hotel room at the resort, set down her suitcases, went over to the sliding-glass door, and walked out onto her lanai. She inhaled deeply, savoring the smell of the ocean. As she exhaled, tension left her shoulders, and she noticed a sweet smell in the air. It was the plumeria blossoms used to make the beautiful flower leis. Janine stood looking over the vast ocean and felt relief, even just for a few moments, from her ever-present stress and anxiety. *I love this view. I could stay here forever.*

She hesitated a few moments before deciding whether to join

the rest of her crew down at the pool bar. She didn't normally like to socialize with the other flight attendants, but she decided to make an exception in this case because the captain had personally invited her to join them. Janine changed into her white Bermuda shorts, flip-flops, and V-neck T-shirt, then walked down to the pool bar. Her crew was easy to find because they were sitting at a big table and already laughing and drinking.

Kerri waved to her and smiled. "You're one round behind us. You're going to have to catch up. What would you like to drink?"

"What do you recommend?"

"They make a fabulous mai tai here."

"Then I'll try that."

Once her fellow flight attendants had a few drinks in them, they started telling stories about some of the crazy pilots they'd flown with.

"Do you remember that wacky guy from San Fran who used to cover himself in cloth napkins because he was afraid of solar radiation?"

"Yes. He was so weird. He'd ask me for hot tea in two cups, filled only halfway, and served on a tray. His hands shook so bad he'd spill any other kind of drink." They all howled with laughter, remembering flying with him. Janine just listened but didn't join in.

"Did you ever fly with this guy?" Kerri asked.

"No. I've only flown out of the West Coast for a few months." She decided to try to join in on the fun and said, "We did have this one strange guy in Chicago that everybody talked about."

"What's the dirt on him?" one of the other flight attendants asked.

"Well, he was a swinger who liked to hit on everyone. Male or female, it didn't matter. He was a short, bald guy, and no one liked to fly with him."

They continued to laugh and regale each other with more funny stories of pilots and passengers. The beautiful Hawaiian sunset in the background, the delicious drinks, and the friendliness of her crewmates made Janine feel welcome and included. She surprised herself by actually enjoying the evening relaxing with them.

"Are you guys ready to go get some Maui tacos?" They all got up to leave.

"Coming with us, Janine?" Kerri asked.

"No, but thanks. I want to walk on the beach for a little bit. See you guys tomorrow." Janine stood up and left the group, walking toward the shoreline, where the white sand beckoned her.

Kerri watched Janine leave the group and couldn't help but stare at her shapely form in her white shorts. She was stately and walked with grace and poise. She'd let down the French twist of her blond hair, and the trade winds made it blow seductively. Kerri could sense that Janine was guarded when she first sat down, but she was happy to see her open up and tell stories with the rest of them. Not just her beauty caught Kerri's attention, but something else about her was mysterious and alluring. She was very curious to know what it was.

❖

Friday, May 2

Kerri woke up early the next morning. She loved mornings on the beach. Most of the tourists were still in bed, the Hawaiian birds were singing, the ocean looked smooth and calm, and the air smelled sweet. She couldn't explain why the air in Hawaii was different. It just was. It felt soft and gentle, and she inhaled deeply. Then she put on her shorts and tank top and headed down to the beach, holding her flip-flops in her hand so she could feel the sand between her toes. The pristine white beach of Maui extended before her for miles. She could walk forever in this paradise. She was light and happy, lacking only a woman to share this with. Kerri glanced at her watch, then turned back toward the resort, because she had a reservation at nine a.m.

Walking by the palm trees near the pool, Kerri saw Janine lying on a chaise lounge on the beach. Wearing a navy-blue Speedo bathing suit, her long legs crossed at the ankles, she was reading a paperback novel. Kerri thought about leaving her alone, but then, on the cover of her book, she noticed a picture of two women holding hands. Before Kerri could decide whether to speak to her, Janine must have sensed her approach and looked up. "Good morning, Kerri."

"Hi. Good morning to you too." Kerri felt like she'd been caught stealing a glance at Janine.

"This place is so beautiful, I can hardly believe it."

"I know. This is one of my very favorite layovers. What are your plans for today?"

"I'm not sure. Anything you recommend?"

"Well, I'd start with the hotel breakfast buffet. They have the most wonderful fresh fruit. I'm headed there now. Want to join me?"

Janine hesitated, then answered. "Yes, I would."

"Great. I think you'll really like it."

Kerri made small talk as they enjoyed their breakfast together.

"So what is all the great stuff here? What are you doing today?" Janine asked.

"Snorkeling off the island of Molokini."

"Where's that?"

"Just offshore, a little south of here. If you come over here to the railing, you can see it." Kerri led Janine to the edge of the breakfast area and pointed to what looked like a crescent moon of rock sticking up out of the ocean. "It's a marine sanctuary in the crater of a small, dormant volcano. The water is crystal clear, and the fish are beautiful."

"Wow. That looks interesting."

"Care to come with me? It's very reasonable, and the boat dock is just next door to the resort."

"Well, I don't know." Kerri could hear hesitation in Janine's voice. Even though she was very happy doing things by herself, Kerri realized she really wanted Janine to join her.

"Since this is your very first layover in Maui, how about if I treat you? I think you'll really enjoy this."

Janine looked at her for a moment, smiled, then said, "Sure, why not?"

Kerri smiled and gave her a fist bump.

Janine and Kerri walked toward a brightly colored catamaran resting in the sand on the shore. A few other people were already on board, and a big Hawaiian man waved to them as they approached the boat.

"Captain Kerri, aloha!"

"Aloha, Kai. Good to see you again."

"You know him?" Janine asked.

"Yes. I've done this snorkel trip many times. I absolutely love it, and Kai's the best."

Janine was a little nervous, but Kerri's snorkeling experience and friendship with the boat captain made her feel more comfortable. They climbed into the boat, and as they sailed across the ocean to the little island of Molokini, Kai handed out masks and fins. The ocean breeze felt cool on her skin, the catamaran's sail snapped in the wind, and the water was smooth and beautiful. The sunlight danced on the water, making it sparkle. It was the most gorgeous day Janine had seen in a very long time.

As they neared the crescent-moon-shaped volcano, apprehension rose in Janine's throat. She could swim, but she'd never snorkeled in the ocean before.

"Are you okay?" Kerri touched her wrist.

"Ah, sure. I'm fine. It's just really windy out here on the water," she lied. Heat flushed uncomfortably across her skin from her shoulders through her neck. Her reaction always betrayed her when she was trying not to look nervous.

"The water will be very smooth once we reach the marine sanctuary in about fifteen minutes."

Janine was grateful they were nearing the small island.

"Look, everybody. Spinner dolphins off the port side," Captain Kai announced.

She turned to her left and saw at least ten dolphins swimming right alongside their boat, racing the catamaran and leaping out of the water. As they jumped, they spun once or twice in the air before falling back into the water. Janine laughed out loud with delight. She could almost see them smiling as they performed their water show.

"Look, Janine. There's a baby." Kerri pointed to the back of the pod.

"Oh my gosh. It's no bigger than a football, and it has a pink tummy."

"They're so beautiful. That's why I like this trip so much. I always see something new."

A big smile slowly spread across Kerri's face. Obviously she loved being on the water. She looked happy and serene, a very different expression from when she was sitting in her captain's seat.

"Oh, goody. We're getting close." Kerri jumped up, moved to the back of the boat, picked up a heavy rope, and helped the crew secure the catamaran to the mooring ball in the water. Janine could hardly believe her eyes. They were floating in the middle of a volcanic crater, the rocky edges rising from the sea around them. She looked over the side of the boat and spotted all kinds of colorful fish swimming in crystal-clear water. "This is amazing."

"Okay, everybody. Come to the back of the boat to the steps.

Rinse your mask in the defog solution, don't put your fins on until you're on the steps, and we have pool noodle floats if anyone wants one." Captain Kai motioned them all over to the steps.

As she followed everyone to the aft steps, she felt her nervous flush move up her neck again. She really wanted to get in the water, but her anxiety made her hang back.

"Everything okay, Janine?" Kerri was standing right behind her.

"Um, sure. I just need a minute." She was afraid her flushed skin made her stand out like a red beacon.

"Why don't we go in together?" Kerri whispered, a kind look in her eyes.

Kerri sat on the bottom step to put her fins on, then glided into the water, looking back at Janine. When she hesitated to get in, Kerri swam back for her and reached out her hand.

"Come on. The water feels great. I've got you." Kerri took her hand and gently led her into the ocean. She knew she was gripping Kerri's hand hard, but she couldn't help it. She was both scared and excited. "Hey, Kai. Throw me a pool noodle," Kerri called back to the boat. "Stick this under your waist, Janine. Now you don't have to swim. You can just float." The buoyancy of the pool float eased Janine's apprehension. "Why don't you try putting the snorkel in your mouth and just breathing through it for a minute?" Janine put the big mouthpiece in and tried to relax her breathing. "That's it. Now try your mask on."

Janine placed the mask on her face, while Kerri held her hand and led her into the marine sanctuary. When Janine lowered her face mask into the water, she almost inhaled a mouthful of salt water at the spectacular sight. Bright colors exploded as thousands of tropical fish darted around her. The coral underneath her unfolded in a myriad of shapes and colors. She relaxed her breathing and took in all the fish swimming. The canary-yellow tangs, the rainbow-colored parrot fish, and the red-and-black sea urchins gave her a sense of calmness as she floated among them.

Or maybe it was holding Kerri's hand as they swam

together. Her hand was strong but also soft. Janine clutched it as they moved toward the shore where the water was shallow and she was close to the coral. She'd never seen so many different kinds of tropical fish in one place. She seemed to be inside a giant aquarium where she was on display, instead of the fish.

Kerri pointed to a long, slender, silver fish, then excitedly gestured toward the coral. She was pointing to a big Moray eel, black with white polka dots, slowly undulating in the current. She was mesmerized. Half of its body was in a hole in the coral, with the head and neck sticking out. It had a scary face, with a row of sharp teeth, and its mouth opened and closed as it breathed in the sea water. If she was on her own and not holding Kerri's hand, she would've been terrified to run across this creature hiding in the coral. But she felt safe holding on to Kerri while she watched this fearsome, magnificent animal. Then Kerri pulled her in another direction. A dark shape loomed in the water ahead of them, big and slow moving. Kerri stopped them in the water, surfaced, and pulled her mask up to her forehead. "There's a Honu over there," she said as she pointed to the dark shape.

"What's a Honu?"

"A Hawaiian green sea turtle," Kerri said. "It's protected, so we can't get too close, but if we hang back a little, we can see it swim in the water." She put her mask back on her face, laced her fingers through Janine's, and they followed the Honu as it made its way to a sandy beach. They stopped short and watched the big turtle pull itself up onto the sand. It was such a graceful creature swimming in the water, but slow and cumbersome on land. "They like to sun themselves on the beach. Aren't they gorgeous?"

"Yes, she sure is." Janine felt like she was witnessing something unique.

"She? Do you know the difference between a male and female Honu?"

"No. I have no idea. It just looks like a female turtle to me." She knew she didn't make any sense, but she didn't care. She was in the most beautiful place on earth, holding Kerri's hand, and felt at one with the sea and the wild animals surrounding them. Janine took in the vista around her. The view under the water in this volcanic crater was amazing—the sky above, blue with a few puffy clouds floating by, the water warm. She felt happy and carefree for the first time in a very long time. She didn't want this day to ever end. Just then, she heard the whistle from Captain Kai at the catamaran calling them back to the boat. *No, not yet. I'm not ready to leave.*

Janine continued to hold Kerri's hand as they swam back to the boat and sensed Kerri was as reluctant to break their contact as she was. They were the last two to climb back into the catamaran. Kerri got out first and turned to assist Janine out of the water. As Kerri rinsed the salt water off with a hose, Janine couldn't help but notice her shapely body under her rainbow-colored Speedo swimsuit. Kerri had long legs, broad shoulders, and muscular arms. A vision of her gliding through the water with her fins on came into Janine's mind. Kerri swam like she was at home in the ocean and the sea creatures were her friends. *She looks like a beautiful mermaid.*

Janine was exhausted from swimming but so very happy. *What an amazing day. I wish it didn't have to end.*

Kerri handed Janine a towel after she rinsed off. She was so beautiful it was hard not to stare at her. She put on her Ray-Bans so she could steal peeks at Janine undetected. She seemed to be a living statue carved from the finest marble. Her pale skin, blond hair, and ice-blue eyes made her look like Kerri's vision of a Nordic goddess.

After Janine dried herself, she started chattering with other passengers, telling them all about seeing the Moray eel and the Honu. She seemed so happy, and Kerri's heart warmed toward her.

Kerri watched Janine put succulent pineapple into her

mouth and reflected on the day. She adored Maui but always struggled with some melancholy when she was here because she was alone. When she'd stumbled across Janine reclining in that chaise lounge, reading a lesbian romance novel, she'd looked like a dream that might transform into mist and drift away. But then Janine had changed everything when she'd said "Yes" to Kerri's invitation, and gradually they'd grown comfortable with each other—swimming, touching, and holding hands.

The joy on Janine's gorgeous face had kept the melancholy far away from Kerri today.

CHAPTER FOUR

When they returned to the marina at the hotel and got off the catamaran, Janine heard Kerri's voice behind her. "Uh-oh."

"What's the matter, Kerri?"

"You have a nasty sunburn on your back."

"Oh, no. I must have missed a spot with my sunscreen."

"It's more than just a spot. It's the whole center of your back. Do you have any aloe vera?"

"No, I don't." Janine was starting to feel heat radiate from her mid-back.

"You really need to put something on that burn, or it's going to blister."

"I'll stop at the hotel gift shop and get something."

"Unfortunately, they don't carry aloe-vera gel there. I have some in my bag you can borrow."

"Thanks, Kerri."

Janine followed Kerri back to her hotel room. Normally, she would be uncomfortable in another crew member's hotel room, but she didn't feel that way walking into Kerri's tidy room. Kerri's uniform hung in the closet, her black suitcase lay open on the luggage stand, and even the bed was made.

Kerri walked into the bathroom and came out with a small plastic bottle of green gel. "Here you go. This is pure aloe-vera gel. You should put this on your back every four hours. It really helps with a bad burn."

"Thank you." Janine was truly grateful for the medicine. Her back was really starting to sting now.

"Can you reach your back to put this on?"

"Uh, not really."

"Let me put it on you. Boy, that's getting really red."

Janine handed the gel back to Kerri, turned around, and waited for her to apply it.

"Your shoulders got burned too. I'm sorry. I should have put sunscreen on your back for you."

Kerri's concern touched Janine.

"Why don't you lie down on the bed and pull your bathing suit straps down so I can apply this gel all over the burned area."

Janine hesitated but then complied. After snorkeling together, she trusted Kerri. She went over to the bed, pulled the bathing suit straps off her shoulders, lay down, and waited for Kerri, the skin of her back throbbing now.

"This'll feel cold." Kerri's voice soothed her. She closed her eyes and took a deep breath. Kerri's fingertips were light at the base of her neck as she smoothed on the cool gel. "Is this okay?"

"Yes." Kerri's gentle hands moved across her burned skin, slowly and methodically, covering every square inch of her tender back. Her touch felt more like a caress than a medical treatment. Janine decided to just relax and enjoy the sensation of Kerri's strong hands gliding over her.

"You're burned to a crisp. I need to apply a second layer of aloe. Is it okay if I lie down next to you while the first layer dries?"

"Sure. Go ahead." Janine felt the weight of Kerri's body on the bed. Her eyelids were heavy from the exertion of swimming, and she drifted off to sleep.

❖

The flaming red skin of Janine's poor back made Kerri feel guilty. *Why didn't I make sure she had sunscreen on? She'll never want to go snorkeling again.*

She touched Janine's skin as softly as she could to spread around the aloe gel. Heat rose from the burned skin. As she smoothed the gel from Janine's neck to her shoulders to her mid-back, her breathing slowed to a steady rhythm. Kerri took advantage of this opportunity to study Janine's body.

The skin that wasn't burned resembled pale porcelain and was as soft as warm silk. She took her time applying the soothing gel, moving her fingers slowly across Janine's shoulders and back. It had been quite a while since she'd touched a woman's body, and she was enjoying the sensation. Seeing the rise and fall of Janine's ribs as she slept next to her, Kerri stopped touching her like she was giving her a medical treatment and started caressing her. She ran her hand up and down the shallow valley of Janine's spine, feeling strong muscles under the hot skin. *What does Janine look like under her bathing suit?*

A small sigh escaped Janine's lips as Kerri continued to soothe her skin. She moved her hand around the perimeter of the burned area and let only the tips of her fingers slide by the side of Janine's breast. A vein the color of lapis lazuli was visible under the skin of her side breast. Kerri suddenly had the desire to drag the tip of her tongue across this vein. *Where is this coming from?*

Kerri banished the thought of licking Janine's breast and continued to smooth on the aloe, letting her eyes drift to the small hollow at the base of Janine's back where the exposed skin stopped and the bathing suit covered her bottom. The thin fabric of the navy-blue Speedo stretched nicely across Janine's firm backside. Kerri had to fight the urge to move her hand lower and squeeze those lovely cheeks. *Down, girl. Down.*

Kerri suddenly stopped touching Janine. She might cross a line she'd regret later. She removed her hand from Janine's back to let the next layer of aloe dry. Lying on the bed beside her, listening to her deep breathing, Kerri simply wanted to rest next to her for a moment. She closed her eyes and dreamt of floating in the ocean, holding hands with this gorgeous woman.

❖

A sound in the distance made Janine slowly open her eyes. The light in the hotel room was starting to dim. *Where am I? What time is it?* She was disoriented and her back hurt. She looked around, surprised to see Kerri next to her on the bed. *Why is Kerri in my room? What the hell happened?* Her shoulders and back were uncovered. *Why am I naked? Oh my God. What have I done?*

Panic started to rise in her throat, but then she moved and felt the sharp sting of her sunburned back. She was actually in Kerri's hotel room and on the bed so Kerri could put aloe on her burned skin. Thankfully, she still had her bathing suit on and wasn't naked after all. She forced the panic back down and made herself breathe.

Janine recalled the amazing snorkeling trip with Kerri and that she'd gotten sunburned. She looked at Kerri's peaceful face as she lay sleeping next to her, appearing so relaxed and content. Kerri made a little sound, rolled toward Janine, then pressed her hip next to Janine's bottom. A small tingle ran from the place where Kerri touched her to her belly. Enjoying the sensation for just a moment, she then realized how completely inappropriate this situation was. She looked at the bedside clock.

"Oh, no. It's forty-five minutes until bus pick-up time. Kerri, wake up. We're going to be late for our show time."

Janine jumped off the bed, pulled up her bathing suit straps, grabbed her stuff, and ran out the door to her own room.

❖

Kerri woke up to the sound of her hotel room door slamming. She looked around, saw that it was dark outside, glanced at the clock, and realized that Janine had left. "Fuck. I have to throw myself together."

She took the fastest shower of her life, crammed her clothes into her roller-board suitcase, hurriedly put on her uniform, and reached for the door handle to leave. "Crap. Where's my hat?" Her round captain's hat sat on the coffee table, where she always put it, along with her airline ID badge. "That's all I need, to forget my damn badge."

Kerri ran down the hall to the elevator and looked at her big pilot's watch. "Shit. I'm five minutes late for the crew bus."

Everyone on the bus was waiting for her. "God damn it, I hate being late," she mumbled to herself. When she boarded the bus, she quickly did a head count to make sure her entire crew was present. She saw Janine sitting in the last row of the bus, looking professional and elegant, and they exchanged a hot look. "Sorry for the delay, everyone. Driver, we're ready to go now."

Kerri's tardiness flustered her, made her feel disorganized and embarrassed. She prided herself on always being prepared and hated not to be. She did a quick inventory of all her essential equipment—cell phone, wallet, airline ID, gun, book bag—sighing in relief that she hadn't forgotten anything. The flight attendants were chatting with each other about their layover activities, and she heard one of them ask Janine what she'd done. Janine answered, "Not much. I just walked around a bit."

Kerri felt slighted that Janine didn't mention the snorkel trip. Maybe it was no big deal to her, though Kerri thought it had been an amazing adventure. Obviously, Janine didn't have the same feelings about the snorkel trip as she did. Kerri shut down that thought since they were turning into the airport and she had to focus on the flight. Nothing could derail her thoughts when it came to preparing for departure.

After they went through security, they had to walk past the crowd of passengers to get onto the jet. Kerri was aware of all the passengers staring at her in her uniform. Many people had probably never seen a woman pilot before, much less a woman captain, and seemed very curious. She checked in with the gate agent, put her bags in the cockpit, then went down the Jetway stairs to flight operations. Kerri and Joe reviewed the flight plan, the weather forecast, the aircraft maintenance status, the fuel load, the weight and balance, the pilot reports, and the passenger count. Everything looked good, so Kerri signed the flight release and was finally able to relax.

Kerri returned to the flight deck and started her preflight checks. This was where she felt most at home, in the captain's seat of her jet. Her hands flew over the knobs and buttons on the overhead panel, the forward instrument panel, and the center console as she checked and set everything for the flight. She could program the flight management computer with the flying route and complete all her checks in fifteen minutes. "Joe, the route's in the box, if you want to check it for me." Kerri watched him review the flight plan point by point to verify the navigation fixes and altitudes.

"Everything looks good to me, Kerri."

"I'm going to brief the flight attendants, and then we'll run the preflight checklist. Do you have your fuel sheet yet?"

"Nope, but it looks like we're getting close to our fuel load."

On the PA, Kerri called all the flight attendants to come forward for their flight briefing. When she stepped back to the cabin, she saw who her chief purser was, and she wasn't pleased. She'd known it wouldn't be George Cato, since he'd flown back on the return leg last night, but she certainly didn't want to see Michelle Hendricks. She was one of the very few flight attendants Kerri couldn't stand.

❖

When Janine heard Kerri's announcement, she walked to the front of the plane for the flight briefing. Kerri delivered the flight information in a very professional manner, though without the same friendliness as during their first flight briefing to Maui. Somehow she sounded different. She provided the required information on the flight time, weather, turbulence, and maintenance status, but her words had a slight edge that Janine hadn't heard before. The chief purser, Michelle, asked a question, and Kerri gave her a very clipped reply, almost like she didn't want to talk to her.

As a flight attendant, Janine had developed a strong ability to read people and their body language. She often encountered international passengers who spoke no English, or kids traveling by themselves, and she had to understand their needs. She sensed some issue between Michelle and Kerri, but she couldn't figure out what it was.

Michelle was competent as a chief purser, but she was no George Cato. She was pleasant and friendly, but she didn't appear to have much enthusiasm for her job. Maybe she was simply tired from having just flown in from LA and now had to stay awake all night for the return trip.

Janine was hoping to have a minute alone with Kerri to thank her for taking her on that spectacular snorkeling trip. She felt bad she'd left Kerri so abruptly in the hotel room when they overslept and almost missed their show time. With all her captain duties, Kerri was much too busy to talk to right now, so Janine would find a few minutes to chat with her once they were enroute to LA and all the passengers were asleep.

Kerri looked so different than she did during their layover in Hawaii. Magnificent in her captain's uniform, she was all business now. No fun and games like when they'd been in the water together. Kerri was very impressive as a captain. She was sharp, on top of everything, confident, and definitely in command of this flight. Janine could see even more clearly how some people could find Kerri intimidating, especially male pilots.

Janine watched Kerri's hands as she talked and felt another tingle in her belly at the remembrance of holding her strong, soft hand in the water. Janine especially liked the memory of her gentle touch on her burned back.

The passengers started boarding; it would be a full airplane for the all-night flight back to Los Angeles. Janine would do a beverage service, and then maybe everyone would sleep for the next five hours. So many thoughts were racing through her mind. She looked forward to a few peaceful moments sitting on her jump seat, without constant passenger interruptions, to process everything that had happened today.

"Flight attendants, please prepare for takeoff," Joe announced over the PA.

Janine double-checked that both left and right aft doors were armed, and she mentally reviewed her emergency evacuation procedures, in case anything happened during the takeoff. She was thankful she'd never had to do a real evacuation, but she practiced the procedure every year during recurrent training. Everything in the galley was stowed, she was strapped in tight to her jump seat, and she nodded to her flying partner, indicating she was ready. As the massive engines came up to full power, they produced their familiar whine. This was her favorite part of flying. The excitement of the takeoff, magically rising into the sky, and the promise of adventure ahead made her love her job.

Janine heard the double ding of the cabin chime signaled from the cockpit. They were climbing past ten thousand feet, and it was safe to leave their jump seats. She and the other aft-cabin flight attendant set up the beverage cart and pushed the heavy cart up the aisle, handing out drinks and snacks. Most people looked exhausted from their Hawaiian vacations, and thankfully, many were already asleep.

After serving all the passengers, Janine glanced at her watch. It was two a.m. California time, and they had three more hours before landing. Janine had a few minutes to relax in her jump seat, and she wanted to relive all the magical sights she'd seen on the snorkeling trip with Kerri. The fish were so gorgeous, and seeing the dolphin pod and the Honu sea turtle had been amazing. Then her thoughts turned to the time she and Kerri had spent lying on the bed together. Kerri had been so sweet to her when she treated her horrible sunburn, which was really stinging now under her uniform dress. This might be a good time to go to the cockpit and chat with Kerri. She pressed the cabin-to-cockpit call button.

"This is Kerri." Her voice sounded very official.

"Hi. It's Janine. Do you guys need a restroom break?"

"Thanks, Janine. Yes. We'll take a break now." Kerri's voice sounded a lot cheerier.

"I'll be right up."

Joe let Janine into the cockpit as he stepped out, and she closed the cockpit door securely behind her. The lights in the flight deck were dim, with a soft reddish glow from all the instruments, and it was pitch-black out the big windows.

"How's everything in the back?" Kerri asked. She was smiling and friendly, completely different than she'd been during the initial flight briefing. "Would you like to sit down?"

Not all captains offered to let flight attendants sit in the copilot's seat, so it was a nice gesture.

"No, but thank you. It kind of hurts my back to lean against a seat."

"Oh, yeah. Sorry. Is it painful?" Kerri's concern appeared genuine.

"Yes. My back's really sore."

"I wish I could put some more aloe on you." Kerri's voice had a sultry edge, and Janine wanted to hear more of it.

"Well, maybe you can, after we land." Janine couldn't stop herself from grinning. She couldn't remember the last time she'd said anything flirtatious to another woman.

A big smile slowly spread across Kerri's face. "I'd like that. My house is ten minutes from the airport. You could come over for coffee, if you like." Kerri looked into Janine's eyes, then reached for her hand and held it, like they were in the water again.

Janine put her other hand over Kerri's and slowly caressed

Kerri's fingers between her hands. *Her hand is so warm.* "I almost forgot why I came up here. I wanted to thank you for taking me on that snorkeling trip. It was amazing."

"You're very welcome. I'm so glad you had a good time. I really enjoyed snorkeling with you too."

Janine stared at Kerri's beautiful lips. They looked so delicious. Then she sensed a slight pull toward Kerri. Was Kerri pulling her hands toward her? Was this some kind of magnetic thing? Whatever it was, Janine decided not to resist. Her lips moved closer to Kerri's, and she saw just the tip of Kerri's pink tongue move across her lower lip. *I want that.*

Janine slowly pressed her lips to Kerri's and was met with the softest kiss she'd ever felt. She opened her mouth for more, and Kerri slid her hot tongue into Janine's hungry mouth. Electric current ran directly from Janine's lips to her belly as a small moan escaped her mouth. Kerri's kiss became more intense. She moved her hand up to Janine's neck and caressed the side of her face as Kerri kissed her fervently. Janine was losing herself in the flood of sensations from Kerri's kisses.

"Ding." They jumped apart. It was the cabin-to-cockpit chime. Kerri reached up to a panel and flipped on the switch for the overhead light. Janine stood up and smoothed out her uniform dress. They were acting like teenagers caught necking.

"Joe's at the door. I'll let him in. Are you stepping back, Kerri?"

"No, thank you."

"Well, I guess I'll see you after landing."

"You sure will." Kerri flashed that dazzling smile again. This would be a long three hours.

CHAPTER FIVE

The scent of Janine's perfume hung in the air after she left the flight deck. Kerri inhaled deeply. Her lips still tingled from the press of Janine's lips. After Joe returned to the right seat, Kerri put the cockpit lights back to the dim setting. The cockpit lights were kept low when flying at night to preserve the pilot's night vision, but Kerri didn't want Joe to see her face turn red as she thought of Janine.

The kiss between them had felt so natural, like they'd been girlfriends for months. Janine's lips were full and luscious. Kerri wanted to kiss them forever. She felt the familiar dampness between her legs. Her body gave her very clear signals when she was attracted to a woman, and she was certainly attracted to Janine. Her firm resolve to never again date a coworker was slowly dissipating. *Maybe it will be different this time.*

Sitting in the darkened cockpit, Kerri allowed her thoughts to drift to what she and Janine might do after they landed in Los Angeles. She would drive them to her favorite breakfast place for blueberry pancakes, then take Janine to her home. She loved her house. It was near the ocean and had big windows so she could see the sky. She would invite Janine to her bedroom, have her remove her uniform dress, then have her lie down for another aloe treatment. If things went as she hoped, she and Janine would make love until they both fell into exhausted sleep wrapped in each other's arms. The mental image made Kerri shiver.

She stared out the big side windows into the night sky. It was truly pitch-black flying over the Pacific Ocean at night, but she had a perfect view of the stars. She could see Orion's belt, Ursa Minor, Cassiopeia, and the Milky Way. When she flew over the North Atlantic, she often saw the Aurora Borealis with its slowly undulating neon colors in the night sky. She wanted to share these beautiful sights with Janine.

Kerri had surprised herself when she and Janine kissed. She prided herself on her professionalism, and having a lip-lock with a flight attendant in the cockpit wasn't exactly proper decorum at work. She wasn't clear who'd initiated the kiss. It seemed like they'd both moved toward each other at the same time. Whoever had moved first didn't matter. The only thing that mattered was the electricity when their lips touched and the connection between them. It was instantaneous and powerful the moment they gazed into each other's eyes. Kerri felt the ache of desire deep within her, and she wanted more.

She turned away from stargazing and checked the time remaining until they reached their next reporting point. She picked up the clipboard with their paper flight plan on it and wrote the required flight data on it. She was tempted to turn the speed knob up to .85 Mach so they would land in LA sooner. But Kerri didn't change the cruise speed because it would cost her an extra three thousand pounds of fuel just to land fifteen minutes early. She was looking forward to her after-flight activities with Janine, but she was still the captain. Nothing would make her compromise the safety of her passengers.

❖

Janine tried to suppress her smile when she left the flight deck. She'd been shocked, and pleasantly surprised, when Kerri kissed her. What an unbelievable day this had been. First, she was on a gorgeous beach in Maui, then she saw the spectacular sea creatures on the snorkeling trip, and now she was kissing the captain on the flight deck.

"You were up there a long time," Michelle, the chief purser, said.

Her comment took Janine off guard. "Yes, well, I was waiting for Joe to come back up."

"Was Kerri nice? Did she talk to you?"

Janine wondered why Michelle was so inquisitive and why she asked such an odd question. "Yes, she was."

"Well, that's good. Kerri isn't always very nice to flight attendants."

"What do you mean?" This remark confused Janine.

"I don't mean anything. It's just that Kerri Sullivan has quite a reputation among flight attendants."

"What kind of reputation?"

"I don't want to talk out of turn, but you should be aware of Kerri's history with flight attendants."

"What exactly are you referring to, Michelle?" Janine was starting to feel concerned.

"Have you heard what Kerri's nickname is in LA?"

"No. What is it?"

"We call her Don Juanita because she's a female Don Juan and she's gone through so many women in LA."

Janine was stunned.

"Look, I'm not trying to say anything bad about her. You're new to LA, and I'm just trying to look out for you, that's all." Michelle reached over and patted Janine's hand.

"I don't understand what you mean. Are you saying she's a bad captain or that she's abusive toward flight attendants?"

"No, of course not. Kerri's a good pilot. It's just that she goes through women very quickly. I want you to be informed."

Janine was very agitated now. "You're talking around something. Please tell me what's going on with Kerri."

"All right, if you insist. One of Kerri's many exes, Brenda Costas, is my best friend, and she got really burned by Kerri."

Janine could hardly believe what she was hearing. This

didn't sound like the lovely woman she'd spent the day with at all. "What happened with them?"

"I don't want to spread rumors, but it's only fair you know the truth about Captain Kerri Sullivan. Basically, she hits on every beautiful woman who crosses her path, especially flight attendants."

"I haven't known Kerri long, but that doesn't sound like her," Janine answered.

"Oh, I see. She's already put the moves on you, hasn't she? Well, you are very pretty. Let me ask you something. Did she invite you back to her hotel room for a back rub? That's her usual first move."

Janine hesitated. "Yes, she did, but that was because my back was sunburned, and she wanted to help me out."

"Sure it was."

Janine sat on the jump seat in stunned silence. *Can this be true?*

"Don't feel bad about going back to her hotel room. A lot of women have fallen for her charms. You're just the next one in a long string of women she's seduced. You're a nice girl, Janine, and I'm trying to protect you from getting hurt like my friend did."

"How did she get hurt?"

"Let's just say she's never been the same since Kerri broke up with her. After Brenda fell in love with her, Kerri dumped her."

"I'm sorry to hear that." The sweet feelings Janine had about Kerri were turning into sadness and anger.

"The worst part was that Brenda transferred to Seattle just so she won't have to run into Kerri."

"That's awful. Is she seeing anyone else now?" Janine felt pity for a woman she'd never even met.

"No, she's not. She told me that, after Kerri, she didn't want to date anyone for a long time. I really miss flying with her." Michelle seemed hurt by her friend's absence.

Janine was really confused and upset. "I better get back to work. Thank you for letting me know."

"Letting you know what?" Karen, the other forward-cabin flight attendant, joined them.

"I was just filling Janine in on our captain's history with LA flight attendants," Michelle said.

"Oh, you mean Don Juanita? Yeah, she's had a very busy dance card. That's for sure."

"Does everyone in LA call her that name?" Janine asked.

"No, not everyone. Just those of us who've been around a while and seen her in action."

"I think Kerri hit on Janine," Michelle informed Karen.

"Oh. Well, just be careful, Janine."

"Thanks. I will. I need to get back to my station."

Janine walked to the back of the plane past the sleeping passengers. Not only did her sunburned back hurt, but her stomach churned with anger. She sat in her jump seat and stared out into the darkness through the small window in the aft-cabin door. Regret descended on her like a heavy weight.

How could I be so stupid? I let her play me like a violin. What the hell was I thinking? With my situation, I can't possibly get involved with anyone. I lost my head momentarily, but I will not allow anyone to use me, certainly not Captain Don Juanita. She's just as bad as those creepy male captains who hit on all flight attendants. I can't wait to get on the ground and off this plane.

❖

"Trans Global 541, contact Los Angeles Center on one-three-two point one."

"Trans Global 541, one-three-two point one. Have a good day," Kerri answered.

Kerri dialed in the radio frequency for LA Center and glanced at the time remaining to their next navigation point. "Los

Angeles Center, Trans Global 541, five minutes from coast in fix at flight level three-seven-zero."

"Trans Global 541, radar contact, squawk two-three-five-one, descend and maintain flight level two-one-zero," the air traffic controller replied.

Kerri set the new altitude for Joe as he started their descent into Los Angeles. It was five a.m., and normally Kerri would be exhausted after being awake all night. But this morning she was wide awake and giddy with anticipation for her post-flight activities with Janine. She hoped Janine was as excited as she was to come over to her home. It was rare for Kerri to invite a woman there, but Janine was different. Something about her was very special.

Kerri couldn't tell what made her special, but she couldn't wait to find out. She wanted to talk to Janine, ask her about her life, and find out if Janine had any feelings for her. Based on the quick kiss they'd shared earlier, she knew Janine was attracted to her, but now she really wanted to get to know her in depth. She had to force herself to put aside her thoughts of Janine and focus on Joe flying the approach into LA. He was very tired too, and this was the perfect setup for him to make a mistake. In the past, after an all-night flight, she'd seen other pilots line up with the wrong runway for landing, set the incorrect navigation frequency, fail to capture the localizer, and even forget to put the landing gear down, all because of extreme fatigue.

After all her years of flying, Kerri had developed the ability to conjure up her last bits of alertness for the approach and landing. She trusted Joe, but she still monitored everything he did. Kerri made the radio calls, checked the altitudes on the arrival, ran the landing checklist, and watched Joe fly the jet. Like many of the first officers, he tended to keep the airplane fast and high. If he was too fast, they couldn't extend the flaps or gear. If he was too high, he'd never capture the glide slope, and they would have to go around.

Kerri knew precisely what their altitude and airspeed should be to safely make a stabilized approach and landing. She allowed the copilots as much latitude as possible to see if they would recognize and correct their own errors, but she would never let them put the airplane in an unsafe position. Kerri would drop a friendly hint by saying, "Looks like they're setting you up for a slam dunk." If they didn't take the hint, she would become more directive and tell them to pull the power to idle, slow the jet, and put the gear and flaps down. She would intervene before the copilots did anything unsafe, then debrief them when they were safety on the ground. She didn't care about bruising their male egos.

The majority of the copilots did a good job flying, and she got along well with almost all of them. Only one little ass-wipe punk, Jonathan Rindell, hadn't listened to her. Flying into Sacramento one foggy night, he was way too high, and he'd failed to slow the aircraft down or configure the jet for landing. Kerri had tried to give him directions, but he didn't comply with her commands. She'd had to take control of the airplane and use all her skill and cunning to get the jet safely on the ground.

After landing, Kerri had tried to explain what he'd done wrong, but he'd refused to listen to her and left the cockpit. She'd called the chief pilot in Los Angeles and promptly had him removed from the rest of her trip. She never knew what happened to this guy, but he was no longer in LA or with the company. Captain Kerri Sullivan did not tolerate insubordination from anyone.

CHAPTER SIX

Janine completed her before-landing duties after she heard Kerri announce the seat-belt sign coming on over the PA. She and her flying partner picked up the last of the cabin trash, secured everything in the aft galley, and buckled in tight to their jump seats. As she heard the landing gear come down, she looked out the small window in the aft door and saw the pale colors of a new sunrise. Ordinarily, she liked seeing a new day dawn after an all-night flight, but today she felt only disappointment.

What had started as a great layover in Maui had turned into a pathetic scene of deceit. She was angry at Kerri for toying with her emotions, but more than that, she was furious with herself because she hadn't figured out she was being played. The realization brought back awful memories of someone else using her. She forced herself to block those painful recollections.

Janine needed to remove herself from this situation as soon as she could after they landed. The copilot was flying the landing, since Kerri was making the PA announcements, and Joe made a very firm touchdown. The airplane slowed down, and the thrust reversers made a loud roar. As soon as all the passengers got off the plane, she would make her escape and, hopefully, never run into Kerri again.

They pulled up to the gate, the seat-belt sign was turned off, and all the sleepy passengers got out of their seats. Janine disarmed the emergency escape slides on the two aft doors, checked her station one last time, and retrieved her black crew bags. She prayed Kerri was still in the cockpit finishing her post-flight duties so she could make a clean getaway. Fortunately, the 767 used two aisles to disembark, so she just might make it off the jet without running into her.

Janine said a quick good-bye to the other flight attendants, and then, instead of walking down the Jetway with everyone else, she opened the door to the exterior Jetway stairs and, carrying her bags, ran down the metal steps in her high heels as fast as she could. She saw the crew bus approaching, hurried to catch it, climbed on board, looked back at the jet one last time, and let out a sigh of relief.

❖

"Brakes set. Parking checklist, Joe." Kerri wanted to finish her after-landing duties as quickly as possible so she could meet up with Janine.

Just as Kerri was closing her flight bag, she heard the master warning system, "Ding." She looked up at the center panel and saw Hot Brakes annunciated on the display.

"Damn it." Kerri picked up the hand mike. "Maintenance, this is 541 at gate seventy-six. We have hot brakes. Confirm wheel chocks are in place."

"Copy hot brakes, 541. Yes, main wheels are chocked. You are cleared to release the parking brake. We'll get the brake fans over to your gate right away."

"Thanks, Maintenance."

"Sorry about that, Kerri," Joe said sheepishly. "I guess I stepped on the brakes too hard."

Kerri was pissed at him, because now they had to make a maintenance write-up and have the brakes inspected. She took a breath and made her voice calm. "It's okay, Joe. Just remember the 767 has very strong brakes compared to a 737, so you need only light pressure on the toe brakes. I try not to touch them until we've slowed below one hundred knots on landing. As soon as you feel the main wheels touch down, pull up the levers into full reverse thrust, and let them do the work for you."

"Okay, Kerri. Thanks."

By the time Kerri put the maintenance write-up in the logbook, packed her flight gear, and secured her gun, all the passengers and flight attendants were already off the plane. She hurried down the Jetway into the terminal looking for Janine, but only the gate agent remained. Then she realized she didn't have Janine's phone number. It was a long shot, but maybe she was waiting for her outside of Flight Operations. She walked as fast as she could to Operations, but Janine was nowhere around. Kerri was sure they'd been clear about their after-landing plans and couldn't figure out where Janine was. Maybe she could find her in the employee parking lot. *I don't even know if she lives in LA or if she commutes to some other city. Why didn't I ask her where she was from?*

After wandering around the lot for twenty minutes, Kerri knew she wouldn't find Janine and resigned herself to going home alone. She didn't stop at her favorite breakfast place. After being awake all night, she just wanted to climb into bed and sleep. She kept replaying that lovely kiss with Janine in the dimly lit flight deck.

Had inviting Janine back to her house been too forward? Everything with Janine in Maui, and on the jet, had felt so natural. Maybe she was fooling herself by thinking Janine might be interested in her. It wasn't the first time Kerri had pursued a woman who didn't feel the same way about her. She hoped she'd learned something from her previous experiences, but clearly she'd misread things with Janine. Reluctantly, she gave up and went to bed, pulled the curtains to make the room black, and tossed and turned before exhaustion overtook her.

I hope I fly with her again.

❖

Janine threw her bags into the trunk of her car and sped out of the employee lot. There was little traffic at five thirty in the morning, and she soon pulled into the driveway of her small bungalow in El Segundo. She tried to be quiet as she entered the tidy house, but then she heard the sweetest sound in the world. "Mommy, are you home?" She couldn't help but smile at the little high-pitched voice of her daughter, Molly.

Janine pushed open the door to her brightly colored room and knelt by her bed. "Why aren't you asleep, Pumpkin?"

"I knew you were coming home, and I just woke up." She held up her little arms for a hug. All the distress of the last few hours in the plane melted away as Janine embraced her tiny five-year-old daughter. Her small body was warm, and she smelled sweet when Janine wrapped her in her arms. Molly held tight to her neck.

"Were you a good girl for Mrs. Harris?"

"Yes, I was, but I still think she smells funny. I like Rosa better. She's more fun."

"I know, honey, but Rosa wasn't available this time. You'll see her next week when I fly again. I promise." Janine bent down and nuzzled Molly's neck, rewarded, as always, with a delightful giggle from her ticklish daughter.

"Mommy, why do you have to go away so much? I don't like it when you're gone." The twinge of sadness in her little voice broke Janine's heart.

"I know. I don't like being away from you either, but I have to work. We need the money. It'll be better when I get more seniority in LA. Then I can do one-day out-and-back trips."

"What if Daddy gave us money? Could you stay home with me then?"

Tears welled up in Janine's eyes at such an innocent and straightforward question from her very smart little girl. "Molly, we talked about that, remember? We can't take any money from Daddy because it would cause some very big problems. We're fine, just you and me. I'm really tired and need to go to bed now."

She knew Molly wouldn't be satisfied with her answer and would bring up this subject again later.

"I'll move over, and you can sleep in my bed with me, Mommy."

"Good idea. First, let me tell Mrs. Harris she can go home, and then I'll come right back." As she started to get up from her daughter's bedside, she heard Mrs. Harris go out the front door and say "Good-bye" on her way out.

Janine took off her high heels and blue uniform dress, then climbed under the covers with Molly. The twin bed was cozy as Molly snuggled up next to her and put her head on her shoulder. Janine exhaled a deep sigh, overcome by bone-numbing fatigue. She squeezed Molly tighter. *This is bliss. I don't need to be in bed with anyone except my angel, Molly.* Janine gently kissed Molly's forehead as darkness and oblivion descended on her.

❖

Kerri slept only a few fitful hours after her all-night flight, preoccupied with thoughts of Janine. She had no clue as to why Janine hadn't waited for her at the end of their flight. Maybe she'd completely misread the situation. But what about that kiss—that amazing, brief kiss with Janine on the flight deck. Kerri closed her eyes and relived that vision.

She remembered Janine in her slightly snug uniform dress leaning down over her as she sat in her captain's seat, Janine's full lips moving in slow motion toward her mouth. The sensations running through Kerri's body were almost too much. Janine's lips were so soft. Kerri recalled sucking Janine's lower lip like it was a luscious, juicy peach right off the tree. Then she felt just the tip of Janine's hot tongue slide between her own lips. Electricity tingled down her spine and into the pit of her belly.

Instead of letting this memory of a kiss with Janine turn into a full-blown sexual fantasy, Kerri jumped out of bed, frustrated and antsy.

She stomped into her kitchen and made herself a double espresso. She never kept much food in the house since she was gone half the time, but she always had excellent coffee from Costa Rica. As she recalled the details of her trip to Maui with Janine, she had to accept the reality that Janine had ditched her after landing. The reason *why* she got ditched preoccupied her thoughts for most of the day.

Had she come on too strong after their snorkeling trip? Kerri hadn't intended to hit on Janine. She'd merely wanted to soothe her skin, but Janine might have misinterpreted her actions. Kissing Janine on the flight deck was probably a bad move, clearly unprofessional. Maybe she'd offended her.

She needed to talk to Janine about this situation. She refused to let problems fester, whether she was dealing with a crew member or a potential girlfriend. She attacked issues head-on, just like she'd done her whole life. She would figure out a way to get in touch with Janine and either apologize for her behavior or see if they had any real connection.

Kerri decided to call George Cato to see if he had Janine's phone number. She would contact Janine, and they would simply iron out everything. Kerri felt the old, familiar laser focus engage her mind. She was persistent and determined when she wanted something. That was how she'd gotten through U.S. Air Force pilot training and all the aircraft training courses with Trans Global. Some exes had called her stubborn, but she preferred to see herself as tenacious. When Kerri Sullivan was on a mission, nothing could deter her.

Chapter Seven

Sunday, May 4

"Hello?"

"Hi, George. It's Kerri Sullivan. I need a favor."

"Kerri, my favorite captain. What can I do for you, darling?"

Kerri smiled at the sound of George's deep baritone voice. "I'm trying to get in touch with a flight attendant who worked the Maui flight with us."

"Let me guess. Is it the blond beauty, Janine, who worked in the aft cabin?"

"You know me too well, George. Yes. I was hoping you had a phone number for her. I just wanted to give her a call."

George laughed. "Sure thing, Kerri. Be right back."

Kerri's heart raced as she waited for George to return.

"Sorry, girl, but Janine Case has an unlisted phone number on the domicile roster. I can't help you with this one."

"Damn. Well, thanks for checking, George. Do you have any other ideas of how I can get in touch with her?"

"You could ask a flight-attendant scheduler. Those folks have everyone's number. But talk to Dusty. She works the midnight shift and is the only nice one anymore. Plus, she's family. Kerri, don't be surprised if she won't tell you. They've gotten very strict about security stuff. Good luck, honey."

"Thanks, George. You're the best. Say hi to Doctor Michael for me."

Kerri had a nine a.m. flight to Boston the next morning, but she needed to talk to Dusty. She stayed up late and drove to LAX at midnight to find her. Even though pilots and flight attendants worked together every day, they rarely ventured into each other's respective operations centers. Traditionally, pilots stayed in Flight Operations and hung out with other pilots, while flight attendants stuck to themselves on a different floor in the maze of offices beneath the airport terminal.

Kerri stepped off the elevator at Flight Attendant Operations and looked around the unfamiliar space for the crew schedulers. She saw a big, open room with multiple computer monitors and phones on each desk and scanned the room for Dusty, even though she had no idea what she looked like. At the back of it, she saw an attractive woman wearing a rainbow ball cap, with the tanned face of a softball player.

"Excuse me. Are you Dusty?"

"Yes, I am. What can I help you with, Captain?" Kerri had worn her uniform on her mission tonight. People tended to listen to her and comply with her requests more readily when she was wearing it.

"I need to get in touch with a flight attendant I flew with on my last trip to Maui. Her name is Janine Case. Could you please give me her phone number and address?"

Dusty paused before she answered. "Is this official business, Captain? You know the rules regarding employee security. I'm not supposed to give out personal information on flight attendants. Sorry I can't help you."

Kerri carefully worded her next question. She didn't want to get anyone into trouble, but she desperately wanted Janine's information. "My friend, George Cato, told me to come talk to only you about this. He said you're the best scheduler, and the nicest one, so that's why I'm here at midnight. I really need to talk to Janine about a personal issue. I promise you, that's all I want. Please, I really need your help, Dusty."

Dusty paused again and looked Kerri up and down. "Well, if you're a friend of George, I might be able help you out just this once." She turned to her computer screen, punched in some keystrokes, and wrote on a Post-It note. She looked around the big scheduling room to make sure no one was watching, then slipped the note to Kerri. "Do not tell anyone I gave you this."

"Thank you, thank you, thank you, Dusty. I owe you big-time." Kerri stuffed the note into her jacket pocket.

"You're welcome, Captain."

"Please call me Kerri. Can I ask you one more favor, Dusty? Can you tell me if Janine is flying, or is she off right now?"

"Stand by." Dusty typed some more, looked at her screens, then jotted something on another note pad. "Here you go. She's flying again in three days on a Kona trip, the afternoon departure. That's all I can tell you, or my ass will be in a sling. They monitor everything we do."

"I understand. Thank you again, Dusty. Here's a little gift for you." Kerri handed Dusty a two-pound box of See's dark chocolate.

"My favorite! Did George tell you I love these?"

"He might have mentioned it. Thanks again." Kerri turned to leave.

"Hey, let me know how everything works out, and thanks for the candy."

"I will. Bye." Kerri tingled with excitement as she glanced at the note with Janine's phone number on it. She couldn't wait to call her.

❖

Janine heard her cell phone ring in the other room.

"Mommy, your phone is ringing."

"Thanks, Pumpkin, but I'd rather stay here with you while you take your bath."

Who could be calling her? Very few people even knew her phone number. Maybe it was the Crew Desk with a flying assignment. They would leave her a message, and she would check it when Molly finished playing in the bathtub.

Bath time with Molly was one of her favorite things in the world. It was more about listening to the stories Molly created with her plastic ocean animals than about getting clean. Molly would sing made-up songs, have fights between the toy dolphins and sharks, and loved talking to her sea creatures. She would play in the water until her fingers looked like little pink raisins. This was one of the few, precious times Molly could play like a regular kid.

Most of the time, Janine was painfully aware of how her child's cerebral palsy made her stand out as different from other little girls. She did everything she could to make life as normal as possible for Molly, which was very challenging, given their situation with Molly's father. Just thinking of him gave Janine the shivers.

"Okay, Mommy. I'm ready to get out."

"Are you all done with your friends?"

"Yes. They're all going to sleep in the water."

"Let me get your towel from the dryer." Janine wrapped her daughter in the toasty towel as she lifted her from the bath and held her on her lap to dry her off. "Ready for your jammies?"

"I can do it, Mommy."

Even though it took Molly quite a while, Janine gave her only minimal assistance in putting on her pajamas. She'd learned years ago that, in spite of her disability, her daughter was a very independent child and wanted to do everything she could for herself. Janine was so proud of her everyday courage. She tucked Molly into bed, kissed her good night, and prayed for her safety.

When Janine checked her phone, she didn't recognize the

caller's number. She got an occasional sales call, but this was a Los Angeles area code, and whoever was trying to contact her had left her a voice message. A chill ran down her spine, so she went to the kitchen and poured herself a glass of wine. Her nerves tightened. Who was calling her and leaving her a message? She ignored the phone as long as she could, and after checking that Molly was asleep, she finally hit "play."

Janine was startled to hear a familiar voice.

"Hi, Janine. It's Kerri Sullivan. I hope you don't mind me getting in touch with you, but I was really hoping we could talk. Maybe I misunderstood, but I thought we were supposed to meet up after our Maui trip. I looked for you but couldn't find you. When you have a minute, please give me a call back. Maybe we could get together for a drink or dinner? Have a great day."

"How did she get my number? Who the hell does she think she is calling me at home on my days off? And, no, I will not be calling you back, Captain Don Juanita." Janine angrily punched "delete" on the message and slammed her phone down. This arrogant woman, who was only looking at her as another notch on her bedpost, had just ruined her beautiful, relaxing evening with Molly. "I hope I never have to see that playgirl again." She went to the kitchen, poured herself another big glass of wine, and tried to calm down.

❖

Kerri anxiously awaited a reply from Janine. She'd felt nervous calling and had tried to sound cheery when she left the message. But she hadn't heard back from Janine, and it was too soon to leave another voice message. Maybe she'd text her later. She didn't want to look too pushy.

After her six-hour flight from LA to Boston, Kerri could barely get to sleep for thinking about Janine. Unlike many layover hotels, the Boston hotel was a grand old establishment with quiet rooms and big, soft beds. Kerri was sure she and Janine had simply had a communication misunderstanding about meeting after their Maui flight. Surely Janine would return her call later.

When Kerri never heard back, she realized she needed to be more direct with Janine. It was time to try again. Hopefully, Janine would answer this time. Disappointed to reach only her voice mail again, Kerri left another phone message. "Hi, Janine. It's Kerri Sullivan again. When you have a minute, please give me a call back. I'd *love* to speak to you. Thanks, and have a good day." She emphasized the word love, to encourage Janine to reply.

After another phone message and three text messages, Janine's lack of response frustrated Kerri. Clearly, she needed to take more drastic measures. Beginning to obsess about Janine, she replayed every word they'd spoken to each other, trying to figure out why Janine wouldn't communicate with her. Did she have a girlfriend at home? Was she not really a lesbian? Kerri's gaydar, and the touch of Janine's lips on hers, convinced her that Janine was the real deal. Straight girls might be curious, but they didn't kiss another woman like that.

Janine must be failing to respond to Kerri's messages for some reason. Whatever that was, Kerri had to speak to her face-to-face. She had to find out the truth. Maybe Janine simply wasn't interested in her. Regardless of the reason, Kerri was going crazy with all her speculation and needed to find out what was up with Janine.

Since Janine refused to reply to her, Kerri decided to call in a favor. She had checked Janine's flight schedule with the information from Dusty and knew Janine was flying the LA-to-Kona, Hawaii trip at four p.m. the next day. She had to act fast if she was going to pull off her plan. She logged into the Trans Global computer system and looked up the crew manifest for flight 401, the LA-Kona trip. Recognizing the names of the captain and first officer, she picked up her phone.

"Hey, Hector. Kerri Sullivan here. I wanted to talk to you about a trip trade for your Kona flight tomorrow."

"Hi, Kerri. What do you have to offer? You know I'm always looking to improve my schedule."

Kerri was sure she could count on Hector's greed, since he had three ex-wives to support.

"How about I take your Kona trip in exchange for my Paris trip? It leaves the same day, you get home earlier, and you'll get paid an extra ten hours of flight time." Since they both got paid by the flying hour, her Paris trip would earn Hector a nice bonus this month.

"You sure you want to give up that trip? You're a lot more senior than me."

"Yes, Hector. I'd like to make this trade, for personal reasons. I need to know if you're interested because I'll have to call the Crew Desk before the trading window closes in fifteen minutes."

"Then pull the trigger, Kerri. I'll take it. And thanks for calling."

"Thanks, Hector. I'll make the change."

"Any time, Kerri. Pleasure doing business with you."

After Kerri called to make the captain change on the Paris and Kona flights, she was very satisfied with herself. It was rare for her to go to such lengths to spend time with a woman, but she found something intriguing about Janine that she couldn't let go of.

All right, Miss Janine Case. Try to avoid talking to me when I have you trapped in a big airplane for five hours over the ocean.

❖

Wednesday, May 7

Janine rushed around the house getting Molly ready for school and herself ready for work. She'd never flown to Kona, on the Big Island of Hawaii, and was looking forward to her trip. She would miss Molly, as she always did, but the promise of adventure on her layover made her optimistic. She might rent a car and drive over to Volcano National Park to see Kilauea for herself. She hoped Kerri Sullivan wouldn't make any more annoying calls or text her. She should have gotten the message that Janine was not interested in her by now.

"When will you get home, Mommy?"

"Day after tomorrow, Pumpkin. I'll be home early in the morning again."

"And will Rosa pick me up after school today?"

"Yes, honey, just like always. Are you ready for your math test?"

"Yes, I am. I'm going to get an A again!"

"That's my smart girl."

"Mommy, will you bring me a present from the volcano? Like maybe a piece of real lava?"

"Sure thing, Pumpkin. Let's roll." Molly's request surprised Janine. She never asked for gifts. Janine usually showed her pictures of the places she flew to, and on occasion she'd pick up a small present for her.

As she maneuvered the car through the school drop-off area, Molly waved at her friends. Janine got her wheeled walker and backpack out of the car, and Molly started to go over to them.

"Hey. Where's my kiss?"

"Sorry, Mommy." Molly turned to kiss her.

"I love you to the moon and back, Pumpkin. Have a great day at school. I'll see you day after tomorrow." Janine held her tight and kissed her.

"I love you more, Mommy. Don't forget the lava rock, okay?"

"I won't." Janine watched her sweet, feisty little girl push her walker over to her friends, her heart catching at the sight of Molly laughing out loud. She still felt a twinge of sadness when she dropped Molly off at school. She loved Molly so much, her chest hurt.

After running a few errands, Janine got her bags together, put her uniform on, and headed over to LAX. She'd reviewed the crew manifest the day prior and saw that she was flying with George Cato again. She didn't know anyone else on the crew, but she assumed they all would be friendly and easy to work with.

When she reached Flight Attendant Operations, Janine checked her company mail and made sure her flight attendant manual was current. Her crew assembled in the briefing room for the duty assignments from George. The more senior women had flown together many times, and they requested to work in the main coach cabin together.

"That leaves you up in First Class with me, Janine." George said.

"Sounds good to me, George." Even though they had fewer passengers to serve in First Class, many flight attendants didn't like being there because it entailed a lot more work. This was especially true when dealing with the prima-donna first-class passengers who acted like they owned the world. Janine didn't care which cabin she worked. She just wanted to do a good job and keep everyone safe.

After the flight attendant crew boarded the airplane, Janine started her safety duties. She checked the door pressure gauges for the escape slides, confirmed that all the fire extinguishers were good, inventoried the medical kits, and inspected the emergency equipment in the overhead bins. Everything looked perfect, as always.

George was busy setting up the galley for his five-star service, and then he decorated the lavatory with his Hawaiian decorations and flowers from home. Again, Janine was amazed at how he could whip together real elegance on a 767.

George picked up the cabin interphone handset and announced in his deep voice over the public address system, "All flight attendants, please come forward for the captain's flight briefing."

When all six flight attendants had gathered in the front of the plane, the captain walked out of the flight deck. It was Captain Kerri Sullivan.

Janine was stunned to see her, since the crew manifest the day before had showed a Captain Hector Gomez as the captain. *Why is she on this flight? Did the original captain call in sick?* Janine could barely listen to her. Kerri's sudden appearance unsettled her, and she had a hard time making eye contact with her. Kerri concluded her remarks with a little joke.

Everyone chuckled except Janine. *She thinks she's real funny. I need to stay away from this arrogant woman.*

Afterward, George asked Janine to take the personalized water bottles up to the cockpit. Janine intended to just set them on the floor for the pilots, but the first officer was getting out of his seat to do the exterior walk-around inspection, so she had to hand them to Kerri.

"Hi, Janine. Thanks for the water. How are you today? It's nice to see you again." Kerri sounded very friendly.

"I'm good, thank you. Here are your water bottles. Do you need anything else?" She turned to leave.

"Hey. Wait a minute. Did you get the messages I left? I was hoping to hear back from you."

Janine hesitated before she answered. She wasn't sure how to handle this situation. She could slap down a pushy male captain in a second, if required, but Kerri was different. She had a hopeful expression as she waited for Janine's reply. She also had that blazing smile and those soft, delicious lips. "Yes, I got them. How did you find my phone number? It's supposed to be unlisted."

"Well, I, um…"

Just then George announced over the PA, "Passengers boarding."

"I have to go." Janine turned and abruptly left the flight deck.

The first-class passengers always boarded the airplane first. Several of them handed her their jackets to hang up like she was a hat-check girl. George recognized many of them, since they were frequent flyers, and gave them their drinks as soon as they sat down.

This would be a full flight, with all two hundred and forty seats occupied and several lap children. Janine liked seeing the families with kids traveling together for a fabulous vacation in Hawaii. She noticed one particularly loud passenger and his wife sitting in First Class. The man in the expensive suit was busy talking on his cell phone as he sent their two kids to sit by themselves in the back part of the coach cabin.

"Hey, George. See that guy in 3B? Do you know him?"

"Yes. That's Mr. David Shapiro. Why do you ask?"

"Well, he just sent his kids to the back of the plane while he and the wife sit up here in First. That just seems odd."

"Oh, honey, that's nothing, compared to what I've seen from these Firsties. He's just a prima donna, that's all. I'll take care of him."

After all the passengers boarded and the gate agent shut the aircraft door, Janine and George armed the forward cabin doors, checked that everything in the galley was secure, then stood in the aisle to do their safety demonstrations. It annoyed Janine that most of the passengers didn't even look at her when she was showing them how to don the life vest and where the emergency exits were. They were too busy playing games on their phones to pay attention to this critical safety information. After their demos, George and Janine sat down next to each other in their jump seats.

"I thought I saw a different captain's name on the crew manifest. Do you know why Kerri Sullivan is on this flight?"

"No, darling. I don't. Maybe the original one's on sick call, or maybe Kerri traded with him. Either way, she's an excellent captain, and I always like being scheduled with her. Don't you like flying with her?"

"No. That's not it, George. I just didn't expect to see her."

As she waited for the airplane to start the push back out of the gate, Janine realized she couldn't do anything about having Kerri as their captain. She would just do her job, try to minimize their contact, and stick to herself during the layover in Kona.

CHAPTER EIGHT

Kerri started to get up out of her seat to go after Janine and talk to her, but the fuel guy was blocking the cockpit door. "Here is your fuel sheet, madam."

She took the piece of paper from him and sat back down in her seat, scanning it with practiced efficiency to verify the gallons of jet fuel boarded and check the balance in the wing tanks. "This looks good. Seventy thousand pounds of fuel on board. Has anyone ever told you that you have the neatest printing of any fueler out here?"

"No, madam. If you have no further questions, I'll leave." He turned abruptly and walked away.

Kerri handed the fuel sheet to her first officer, Ray Elliott, so he could confirm the fuel load. "Look how tidy his handwriting is, and he didn't even get any gas on the sheet."

"Yeah. That's about the cleanest fuel guy I've ever seen. Most of them smell like a gas station. Looks good to me, Kerri."

They both went about their preflight duties, Kerri glancing at Ray as he completed his checks. She hadn't flown with him before. He was new to the airline and to flying the 767. He was still wearing the lapel pin of a pilot on first-year probation. However, she wouldn't tell him what to do unless he asked for help, even though he was somewhat slow entering the required information in the flight management computer.

Kerri decided to let Ray fly the leg to Kona since it didn't have a demanding arrival or a short runway. In fact, Kona was a great airport to land at because it had a nice long runway on a big, flat section of a lava field, it was easy to see the airport from the air, and there was no high terrain near the airport. It was the perfect place to become comfortable landing a big jet.

"I have the flight plan in the box if you want to check it."

"Thanks, Ray." She compared her paper flight plan with the points in the navigation computer, verified the correct latitudes and longitudes, and then typed some additional information into the box.

"Did I miss something?"

"We need to include the altitude change when we step from thirty-four to thirty-six thousand feet so the flight computer will give us a more accurate fuel estimate. You also want to select an arrival and runway for landing. Other than that, everything looks good."

Kerri didn't have to tell him she was watching everything he was doing and checking his work. Just by her actions, she showed him she was thorough and would catch his errors, but she wouldn't be a jerk about it. She wanted him to know she ran the crew like they were a team and that she welcomed his input. He would encounter the few asshole captains on this fleet soon enough and learn that Kerri wasn't one of them.

"How do you like to do the HF radio checks?" Ray asked.

"Call Clearance Delivery and ask for the primary and secondary frequencies. Then you just need to make sure we can receive and transmit on both freqs." Kerri was glad he felt comfortable enough to ask her techniques. They would work together well and have a good flight today.

Kerri was still hoping to grab a minute with Janine before they pushed back, but the gate agent showed up ready to close the airplane door. Maybe Janine would come up and talk to her after they were airborne.

❖

The appearance of Kerri as the captain on this flight still unsettled Janine. Regardless of how she felt about Kerri, George Cato was a very professional chief purser with a very high standard of service, and she had to step up her game to keep up with him and the first-class passengers.

Once all the passengers and bags were settled and the doors were armed, George walked up to the flight deck. "The cabin is secure, Captain, and we're ready to go."

Janine sat next to George in their jump seats as they taxied out for takeoff.

After a brief ten-minute taxi, Ray called out over the PA, "Flight attendants, please prepare for takeoff." This was their last chance to make sure no passengers were out of their seats and everything in the cabin was ready. They were both quiet, mentally reviewing their emergency-evacuation procedures.

George whispered to Janine, "I still love the takeoff the best."

"Me too."

After the jet gracefully lifted into the air, she waited for the sound of the landing gear coming up because that meant everything was good with the airplane. Both she and George stayed in their seats until they heard the familiar double-ding from the cockpit. They were passing ten thousand feet, and it was safe to get up.

George was a study in motion and efficiency as he set up the galley to serve dinner to eighteen people in a space the size of a large hall closet. Janine watched him closely to copy his techniques the next time she flew as chief purser. He clued her in on some of the idiosyncrasies of the passengers.

"In addition to Mr. Important in 3B, watch out for Mrs. Ellis in 5C. She's never satisfied with the cabin temperature and will bitch about it for the next five hours."

"How do you handle that, George?"

"I just keep refilling her wineglass, tell her I'll inform the cockpit, and eventually, she'll doze off. Simple."

"You make it look so easy."

"Well, after forty-two years, I've learned a few tricks along the way."

Janine watched George weave his magic spell over all the entitled, spoiled, wannabe big shots in First Class. *I don't know how he keeps that big smile on his face, but he is impressive.*

❖

"Trans Global 401, Los Angeles Center, proceed direct to coast out fix, FICKY, and switch to enroute advisory frequency."

"Los Angeles Center, Trans Global 401, direct FICKY and switching to enroute frequency. Aloha," Kerri answered.

"Why did dispatch put us on this route, Kerri? It seems pretty far south and not very direct."

"Good question. Take out your weather charts and look at the twelve-hour significant-weather forecast."

Ray did as Kerri asked and looked at the charts, but he didn't say anything. He appeared confused.

"See that big thunderstorm system near North thirty and West one-forty? We use the Hawaiian Track System with one-way routes over the ocean, so to avoid that weather, dispatch has us on one of the southern tracks. We should be well clear of any turbulence from that system."

"Oh, yeah. That makes sense. Thanks for showing me."

"Any time, Ray. I'm going to run the cruise checklist and write the estimated crossing times for our nav fixes on the flight plan."

Kerri completed her instrument and fuel checklists with practiced efficiency. She had the list memorized, but she referred to it anyway, just to make sure she hadn't missed anything. Everything looked perfect, just the way she liked it, and they would land fifteen minutes early. Kerri also calculated she could save an extra two thousand pounds of fuel by staying at a lower altitude with less headwinds.

After completing her paperwork, she pushed her captain's seat all the way back to stretch out her long legs and get comfortable for the next four hours. She then took a few moments to gaze out the big windows of her 767. The deep-blue Pacific Ocean stretched endlessly before her, a layer of soft, fluffy white cumulus clouds beneath her. She felt most at home here. When she was in the sky flying her jet, with the beautiful horizon before her, all was right with the world.

Kerri loved commanding her magnificent airliner and was intensely aware that she held the lives of two hundred and fifty passengers and crew in her hands. She was honored to accept this huge responsibility.

"Ding." The cabin-to-cockpit chime sounded.

"This is Kerri."

"Are you guys ready for your crew meals?" George asked.

Kerri wasn't particularly hungry, but Ray vigorously nodded.

"Sure, George. You can bring those up now."

The chime sounded again a few minutes later. "I'll get the door." Kerri rose from her seat, kept her right hand on the grip of her holstered gun, checked that the area in front of the door was clear, then opened the door.

She was surprised to see Janine standing before her instead of George.

"Well, hi, Janine."

"Here are your meals. Do either of you need to step back?" Janine barely looked at her. She sounded officious and appeared to be in a hurry to return to her cabin duties. Kerri now understood why some of the other flight attendants called her the Ice Queen. She could radiate cold like an iceberg when she wanted to.

"No. We're fine. Thanks for bringing the meals up."

Janine gave her the food trays without comment, then firmly closed the cockpit door.

Kerri handed Ray his meal, then sat down at her seat, balancing her tray on her knees. Janine's demeanor puzzled her. How had things changed so quickly? They'd had such a great time on their Maui layover, as well as on the flight deck in the middle of the night flying back to LA. Maybe calling her and texting hadn't been such a great idea. Janine might think she was some kind of stalker. Also, Kerri did feel a little guilty about bribing Dusty to get Janine's phone number.

Kerri completed her required position reports and recorded the time and fuel remaining as they crossed each navigation point on the paper flight plan. Her non-flying duties weren't particularly exciting as they droned across the water, and sometimes she chatted with her first officer, but Ray was busy wolfing down his meal. Instead, Kerri allowed Janine to occupy her thoughts for the next two hours.

As Kerri looked down from her big side window to the sparkling water beneath them, she wondered what it would feel like to walk along the beach holding hands with Janine. It was a small fantasy, yet it stirred strong feelings in her heart. It had been so long since she'd enjoyed such a simple pleasure as holding hands with a woman she truly cared about.

She wasn't thrilled that she'd been through so many women in her lifetime. She'd never wanted to have many girlfriends, but somehow her relationships never seemed to work out. Kerri really was just a hopeless romantic who wanted to fall in love with a woman who was also in love with her. Maybe Janine still could be that person. But first, Kerri had to apologize to her.

❖

"Is the cockpit door latch sticking, Janine?"

"No. I don't think so. Why do you ask?"

"Well, you kind of slammed the cockpit door after you gave the pilots their meals, and I wondered why. Maybe the door isn't the problem?" George asked with a sly smile.

"Sorry. I didn't mean to slam it. And, no, there's not a problem." She quickly left the forward galley before George could ask any more uncomfortable questions.

She tried her best to put on her smiling work face as she moved about her section. Underneath her outside smile, she was disconcerted about Kerri Sullivan, and she had to admit that she felt off balance. She was still very annoyed that Kerri had called her at home and that she didn't take the hint that Janine wasn't interested.

Whatever she felt about Kerri, she had to put that aside and focus on her job. All the first-class passengers had been fed and were busy watching movies or sleeping. She glanced at her watch, noting they had a little more than two and a half hours to go. She resolved to try to avoid any more contact with Kerri during the rest of the flight. Maybe she'd get a chance to talk to her privately on their layover to tell her to stop with the calls and texts.

Just then she heard the cockpit call chime, and she picked up the handset to answer.

"We're done with these food trays and I'd like to step back for a restroom break," Ray said.

"Okay. I'll be right up."

Janine didn't want to go back into the flight deck and face Kerri again. "George, would you do it?"

"I would, honey, except Mr. Important is ringing his call button again. Go ahead. It'll be fine."

Reluctantly, Janine pressed the cabin-to-cockpit call button. Ray opened the cockpit door, let Janine in, then he entered the cabin. Janine checked that the cockpit door was securely locked behind her and turned to Kerri.

"Would you like to sit down?" Kerri gestured to the first officer's seat.

"No, thank you. I prefer to stand." Janine didn't want to sound curt, but she was also very uncomfortable being on the flight deck with Kerri, though this time it wasn't in the middle of the night. Now bright sunshine streamed through the panoramic windows, and the beautiful blue ocean horizon stretched before them. At home, Janine had refused to respond to Kerri's phone calls or texts over the last several days. But in this situation now, trapped on the flight deck with her, she had nowhere to run.

Kerri gazed into Janine's eyes for a long second. "I was really hoping to talk to you. You and I must have gotten our wires crossed. I certainly don't want to bother you, and if you're not interested, I'll understand, but I would like for us to at least be friends and be able to work together well."

Kerri sounded sincere, and some of Janine's apprehension melted. "I'd like that too."

Kerri reached for Janine's hand and smiled at her.

"Ding." The cabin-to-cockpit chime sounded.

Janine broke eye contact. "That must be Ray. Let's talk when we get on the ground. Let me know when you're ready for the door."

Since they were above twenty-five thousand feet, Kerri reached into her left-side compartment, pulled out the required oxygen mask, and placed it on her head. "Sounds good, Janine. You can open the door now."

BOOM!

❖

The plane lurched violently, and the air in the cockpit instantly turned into cold fog. Both of Kerri's ears popped. The warning horn blared, and the red master warning lights flashed. *What the hell was that? We have a rapid decompression!*

She recited out loud the emergency memory steps. "Oxygen masks—ON, 100%." Kerri looked to her left to verify the regulator was set at one hundred percent oxygen. "Crew communication—establish." She looked at her comm panel through the face mask. It was hard to see the small flight interphone switch. She flipped it to the "mask" position, keyed the yoke mike button, and heard her own voice over the cockpit speaker.

Ray had returned to his seat, put on his lap belt and shoulder harness, and was flipping through the emergency checklist. Then he just sat there.

"Ray. Ray. Put your mask on." Kerri reached across the center console and slugged him hard in the shoulder. He turned to her with a dazed expression.

"Mask on, now!" Kerri pointed to her face mask. Ray finally nodded and put on his own oxygen mask.

As Kerri tried to prevent Ray from blacking out from hypoxia, the airplane started to roll to the right. She grabbed the yoke, clicked off the autopilot, and turned the plane to the left. She was losing airspeed rapidly. "What now?"

Kerri quickly scanned the engine gauges. "Oh, no. We've lost the right engine too." She lowered the nose of the jet to regain airspeed and not stall. The words of her first air force instructor pilot came immediately into her mind. *"Fly the jet, fly the jet, fly the jet."*

Kerri stepped on the left rudder pedal to correct the yaw, lowered the nose, and accelerated to single-engine cruise speed. She set the rudder trim and the pitch trim to stabilize the aircraft.

"Ray, are you okay? Silence the warning bell and get out the engine-fail checklist. Because we've lost cabin pressure, I'm descending to ten thousand feet."

"Yes, ma'am. I'm fine. I'll start working on that checklist."

Kerri saw something out of the side of her oxygen mask. It was Janine's blue uniform dress. She was lying on the floor of the flight deck, not moving, her pale face a sickly blue.

CHAPTER NINE

"Ray, you have the aircraft. Maintain the current airspeed and descent rate, and level off at ten thousand feet."

"Yes, ma'am."

Kerri unbuckled her lap belt, slid her seat back, then climbed out of it, careful not to tangle her oxygen cord. She knelt beside Janine and quickly scanned her body, looking for signs of injury or blood. She rolled Janine onto her back, then reached behind her seat to the side oxygen compartment. After she took out the observer's oxygen mask and checked the regulator at 100%, she gently lifted Janine's head and placed the mask over her face. Then, she waited.

"Come on, Janine. Come back to me."

After what felt like an eternity, Janine's eyelids fluttered open. She looked confused as her gaze darted around the cockpit.

"Can you sit up? Let me help you." Kerri placed her arm under Janine's shoulders and pulled her to a sitting position on the floor. "Are you hurt?"

Janine shook her head. "No. I think I'm okay, just dizzy. What happened?"

Kerri looked over her shoulder to the aircraft instruments. "Ray, bring the nose up. You're descending too fast. Keep the speed at two-fifty." She turned back to Janine. "Can you stand up?"

"Yes, I think so. Can I take this off?" She reached for the oxygen mask.

"No. You have to keep it on. We've lost cabin pressure and the right engine. I have to get back into my seat to fly the plane. I need you to sit in the observer's seat and put on the lap belt."

Kerri got Janine into the cockpit jump seat, behind her own seat, buckled the lap belt around her hips, put her hands on Janine's shoulders, and stared into her eyes. "We're going to be all right, Janine."

Kerri climbed back into her seat. "I have the aircraft. What's our status, Ray?"

"Roger. You have the aircraft. We're passing twenty-one thousand feet. Level-off altitude of ten thousand is set, airspeed is two-fifty."

"Let's try to figure out what the hell's going on. First, I have to call the cabin."

Kerri pushed the cabin call button.

"George here. What happened, Kerri?"

"We're still figuring that out. I need you to get a portable oxygen walk-around bottle. Come up to the cockpit and help Janine. She passed out. Use the emergency entry procedure."

"Yes, Captain. I'll be right there."

Kerri turned in her seat and looked behind her to check on Janine. She was still conscious but had a dazed expression. George entered the cockpit and took off the flight-deck oxygen mask, secured the mask from the portable oxygen tank to her face, looped the sling of the walk-around bottle over her shoulder, and then helped her stand up. He tapped Kerri on the shoulder, then gave her an "okay" hand signal as he and Janine left the flight deck. She felt a small relief knowing George would take care of Janine in the cabin. Now she had to focus on her damaged jet.

❖

"Are you hurt?" George asked.

"No. I'm fine." Janine looked down the aisles of the plane and saw yellow oxygen masks dangling from the ceiling the entire length of the aircraft. It looked like most of the passengers had already put the masks over their faces, and the other flight attendants were walking the aisles helping them.

Janine had a headache, but at least she wasn't dizzy anymore. She tried to piece together what had happened. One minute she was opening the cockpit door to let Ray in, and then the plane lurched, the air turned to cold fog, she lost her balance, and she stumbled to the floor. She remembered Ray stepping over her and how she tried to get up, but then everything went blank. The next thing she knew, she was sitting in the cockpit jump seat with a pilot face mask on, and Kerri was telling her everything would be okay.

Clearly, everything was not all right. They had lost cabin pressure, the oxygen masks had dropped, and now the plane was descending. Something was very wrong with this airplane.

"What happened, George?"

"I'm not sure. After you went up to the cockpit, I felt the plane lurch, like we hit something, and then we lost cabin pressure and the masks dropped. We have a window out on the right side, just in front of the wing. It might have been a window failure."

"Are any passengers hurt?"

"Fortunately, no one was in that row. We probably have a few people with scratches from the flying debris, but that's all so far. You were in the cockpit when this happened. What did you see?"

"I can't remember. I heard the noise, saw the fog, and then blacked out. Thanks for helping me."

"I didn't do anything. Kerri took care of you. She got you into the jump seat and put a mask on you."

"Oh, I didn't know that." *Kerri just saved my life.*

"Can you walk? Let's make sure the passengers have their oxygen masks on, and then we'll secure the carts and galleys."

Janine was still woozy, but she was able to focus on her job. Some of the passengers had their masks on wrong, with the yellow rubber cup over just their mouth, not the mouth and nose, as required. A few didn't have any mask on. Instead, they had blue lips and looked like they were sleeping. She went over to one unresponsive man, pulled the cord of the dangling mask to start the oxygen generator, put the yellow mask over his face, and then shook him until he started to come around. Taking a deep breath, she turned to look across the big cabin at all the passengers. Several were crying, and they all looked terrified.

Janine's training kicked in, and she took care of the passengers just like she'd practiced every year in recurrent training. She knew Kerri was descending the airplane to a safe altitude where they could breathe. She'd been through a few emergency situations during the time she'd flown with Trans Global, but nothing like this. She was very aware that the lives of her passengers, and her own life, were in the hands of their captain. She prayed Kerri was as good a pilot as George said she was.

❖

Kerri looked above her head at the overhead panel. All the major aircraft systems were lit up like a Christmas tree, with amber and red warning lights all over the panel. She had to figure out the mechanical status of her crippled jet, and figure it out fast. She knew they'd lost cabin pressure and her right engine had failed, but she didn't know why. She had the airplane in a controlled, stable descent, for now, but she was afraid there could also be a serious structural problem. She needed more information right now.

"Ray, you have the aircraft. I need to talk to George."

"Roger. I have the aircraft."

Kerri pushed the button on her comm panel and called the cabin.

"George here."

"I need to know what happened in the back. Can you tell me what the cabin looks like?"

"Stand by, Kerri. Let me assess the situation, and I'll call you back."

Kerri turned toward Ray. "I have the aircraft. How are we coming on the engine-fail checklist?"

"We've completed the steps to secure the engine, and now we have to decide if we want to attempt an engine restart."

Kerri scrutinized the engine gauges. "We've lost all oil and have zero rotation. This engine is seized, and we can't attempt a restart. We're now single-engine."

"Can we make it the rest of the way like that?"

"This jet's certified to fly on one engine for up to three hours. We just passed the point of equal time on the route, so the closest place to land is Hilo, Hawaii. I'll put direct Hilo in the nav computer." Kerri entered the airport code for Hilo in the box, which read nine hundred fifty-seven nautical miles to fly to Hilo. *Crap, that's a long time on just one engine.* "We'll be okay. Let's continue our analysis. Run the rapid decompression checklist."

As they talked, she could hear the fear in Ray's voice. She not only had to be the captain and fly the jet, but she also had to keep Ray focused on doing his job. She would deal with her own fear later.

"Ding." The cabin was calling.

"This is Kerri."

"It's George, and here's the status of the cabin. The side window in row fifteen is missing. I think that's why we lost cabin pressure. I also spotted three small holes in the side wall near that window. When I looked out the window, I could see the front part of the engine, and it looks pretty torn up and scorched. The oxygen masks are down, and all the passengers are okay. What happened?"

"The right engine must have seized and then disintegrated, which caused shrapnel to puncture the fuselage. That must have broken that window and caused the decompression. We're descending to ten thousand feet, and I'll let you know when it's safe to take off the oxygen masks. We're diverting to Hilo, about two hours away. I'll brief the passengers in a minute, as soon as we finish our checklists. Thanks."

The cabin damage report from George made sense. If the engine tore itself up, it could send sharp pieces of metal into the body of the aircraft.

"How are you coming on those checklists, Ray?"

"Almost complete. As soon as we level off at ten thousand feet, the rapid-decompression checklist is finished. The engine-fail checklist is complete. Since that engine shredded itself, we've also lost the right hydraulic system and the right electrical generator. Would you like me to start the auxiliary power unit so we'll have a backup generator?"

"Yes. Good idea, Ray. Start the APU. Passing eighteen thousand feet, I'll get the exterior lights on. I need to talk to San Francisco Radio, and to flight dispatch, to advise them of our situation. You have the aircraft."

Kerri called on her high-frequency radio but had no response. She decided to try to contact another Trans Global jet on the company interplane frequency.

"Mayday, mayday, mayday. Any aircraft, this is Trans Global 401, declaring an emergency." She waited for a reply, heard nothing, then repeated her message.

"Trans Global 401, this is Trans Global 506. We copy your emergency. Go ahead."

"Trans Global 506, this is 401. We've lost the right engine, had a decompression, and are descending to ten thousand feet. I'm proceeding direct to Hilo. Estimate time to Hilo is two hours. Two hundred fifty-two souls on board. Please relay to company and San Francisco Radio."

"Copy all, 401. I'll call them and give them your information. Any casualties?"

"No. We're all right. Thanks for your help, 506."

"Passing eleven for ten thousand feet," Ray said. He leveled off the jet, pushed the left throttle up to accelerate, and reset the rudder trim. They were stable for now.

"I'm off the air, Ray. I need to brief the passengers." Kerri mentally composed her thoughts before she pressed the public-address button. She needed to reassure her passengers, but she also needed to be truthful with them about how serious this emergency was. She took a deep breath and used her calm, confident captain's voice as she informed them of their situation. Hopefully they would believe her when she told them everything would be all right.

❖

When Janine heard Kerri's voice, she stopped what she was doing to listen. This was the first time she could truly exhale since this emergency started. Kerri's voice was professional, but also comforting, as she told them about the damaged airplane and the plan to divert to Hilo. Janine made eye contact with the other flight attendants, who nodded their relief to each other.

When Kerri announced over the PA that they were at ten thousand feet and could remove their oxygen masks, the passengers seemed to calm down. Even though it was much warmer at ten thousand feet than thirty-four thousand, the cabin was cold, and she handed out all the blankets they had. The passengers started asking for lots of alcoholic drinks, since they were so shaken by what had happened.

"Janine, can you get the medical kit from the back of the plane? We have a few people with cuts."

"Sure, George." All the passengers watched her as she walked down the aisle from First Class to the aft part of the plane. They were obviously afraid and confused, and they needed her to reassure them. She forced herself to smile and touched their shoulders as she walked past them. She could appear brave, even if she didn't feel very courageous right now.

A doctor on board tended to the injured passengers, and

Janine assisted her. The yellow oxygen masks still dangled from the ceiling like spaghetti, and papers were strewn about the entire aircraft. The once clean, sleek interior of the jet now looked like a messy haunted house.

For the first time, Janine realized she was cold. She'd been so busy taking care of the passengers, she hadn't even thought about her own physical condition. Now she became aware that the back of her head hurt.

George came up to her. "Oh, honey, we have to get some ice on your head."

"What is it?"

"You've got a big bump back there. That must have happened when you hit the deck in the cockpit."

"I did?"

"Yes, you did. You also blacked out. Kerri had to put an oxygen mask on your face. Don't you remember? Are you sure you feel okay?" He grabbed a plastic trash bag, put ice in it, and gently placed it on the back of her head.

"Thank you, George. I'm fine."

"We've got everything in the main cabin under control. Why don't you sit in your jump seat for a few minutes? We still have two hours to go."

"Okay." Janine strapped herself into her jump seat and tried not to think about her throbbing head. Instead, she thought of Molly. Her daughter was expecting a phone call from her tonight. She couldn't forget to call her because she would have quite a story to tell. Then her thoughts turned to Kerri.

Chapter Ten

What a relief to take off her oxygen face mask after they leveled off at ten thousand feet. Ray had completed all the checklists, the jet was stable, and their remaining engine was running smoothly. Kerri took a deep breath.

She was worried about her passengers, even though George had assured her no one was badly hurt. As she looked around the cockpit for her paper flight plan, the yellow master warning light came on.

"What now?" Her eyes went to the center display screen, where she read "Fuel Imbalance."

"That makes sense with only one engine running." Kerri reached up to the overhead panel to use the fuel pumps so she could balance the fuel in the wing tanks and stared at the fuel-quantity display in disbelief.

"Ray, tell me what you see on the fuel quantity."

"Center tank is zero, right-wing tank is zero, left-wing tank is five thousand pounds. Total fuel on board is five thousand. What the hell?"

"We're losing gas, and we're losing it fast." She could see the digital display counting down. "The shrapnel from the engine must have punctured both wing fuel tanks."

Not only had Kerri lost an engine and cabin pressure, but now she had a massive fuel leak. She punched some numbers into the flight management computer to confirm the mental math she'd done in her head. The answer was clear. A cold lump settled in her chest.

"We don't have enough fuel to make it to Hilo."

"What are you saying?"

"We're going to have to ditch in the ocean."

A cold, metal hand gripped Kerri's insides. When she was in training, she'd seen disturbing videos of planes trying to land on water, and the attempts usually didn't end well. Either the plane hit the water too hard and broke into pieces, or the aircraft cartwheeled and sank. Kerri couldn't allow herself to think about these images. She had one job to do, and she would focus her mind and her body on that one task. She had to safely land this massive 767 in the middle of the Pacific Ocean.

How much time do I have? She quickly calculated in her head when they would run out of fuel. With only one engine running, she would burn five thousand pounds in an hour. But she didn't have an hour left, not with that fuel leak. Her best guess was thirty minutes until they ran out of gas and fell from the sky. She had to prepare for ditching and land the plane on the water while she still had control of the jet.

"Ray, we have fifteen minutes to get this airplane to a landing on the water."

Ray sat in stunned silence.

"Ray, did you copy what I said? We are doing a water landing in fifteen minutes. Get out the ditching checklist, and let's start working on that."

Still appearing dazed, Ray said, "Yes, ma'am. I'll get on that."

Now Kerri had to brief George, the rest of the crew, and the passengers to prepare for ditching. She paused for a moment before she called him. In her entire life, Kerri never expected to have to make this call.

She pressed the PA button. "George, please come up to the flight deck."

George entered the cockpit and stood ramrod straight as he listened to her describe their emergency situation. Then he nodded when Kerri said they had to ditch the aircraft in the water. "I'll make sure everyone in the cabin is ready when we have to evacuate the airplane, Captain. Do you need anything else from me?"

"No. That's everything. Call me when the cabin's ready. One more thing."

"Yes?"

"Make it quick. We only have fifteen minutes left."

"Okay." George left the flight deck.

❖

"All flight attendants, come forward," George announced over the PA.

Janine walked to the forward galley with the other six flight attendants.

"Captain Sullivan just informed me that we have a fuel leak and we aren't going to make it to Hilo. We have to ditch the aircraft on the water, then evacuate the passengers into the slide rafts. Time remaining, fifteen minutes." George stood silently before them, pausing as his words sank in.

Janine heard comments from her fellow flight attendants, who were clearly nervous and scared.

"George, are we going to be all right?" one of them asked.

"Look. I know none of us expected this when we came to work today, but here we are, in a very serious situation. We've all been trained on ditching procedures and emergency evacuation. The passengers are looking to us to remain calm and to get them safely off this jet and into the slide rafts. You're all professionals, and I expect you to maintain your composure and do your jobs. Go back to your stations, get out your manuals, and let's run our checklists. You have ten minutes left before landing. Let's get to work."

Janine felt like she'd been thrust inside a surreal disaster movie. This couldn't possibly be real. She was trapped in disbelief. She pulled George aside. "Are we really going to make it?"

"Kerri Sullivan is the best captain I've ever flown with in my forty years as a flight attendant. If anyone can land this jet on the water, she can. We have to have faith in our training, just do our jobs, and get everyone off the plane. We're going to get through this, Janine." He gave her a brief hug. "Now, let's get busy. We only have a few minutes."

Inside Janine's head, she was saying, "Oh, my God. Oh, my God. Oh, my God." She forced herself to put a calm expression on her face for the passengers, even though she was screaming inside. She had a lot to do in a very short period of time. She put her head down and performed her tasks as fast as possible.

She picked up the food trays and stowed them in the galley carts. When Janine tried to collect the wineglasses, Mr. Shapiro, in 3B, refused to give her his. She wanted to smash the glass on his self-important head, but she restrained herself. *These people have no idea what's ahead of them. Neither do I.*

Just then, she heard Kerri's voice and stopped to listen.

"Ladies and gentlemen, this is Captain Sullivan. I need to update you on our situation. As you already know, we lost cabin pressure from a window failure. This window broke due to debris from the right engine, which disintegrated and sent metal pieces into the cabin. It looks like the engine shrapnel also punctured both our wing fuel tanks and we have a large fuel leak. We don't have enough fuel to make it to Hilo. Because of this, I will be landing the aircraft on the water. When we come to a stop, we'll be evacuating the aircraft into the slide rafts. I know this situation is very frightening, but it is absolutely essential that you follow the flight attendants' instructions, because your life depends on it."

Janine heard gasps and crying from the passengers as she forced down her own fear. She had a job to do, even if it was the last thing she'd ever do on this earth. She went through the cabin quickly, checking that everyone had their lap belts on. She directed the passengers to reach under their seats, put on their yellow life vests, and stow their loose items. One man continued to type on his laptop computer, ignoring her commands.

"Sir, you need to put that computer away."

"Just a minute," he answered, still typing as fast as he could.

Janine wanted to scream at him to quit being an idiot and put his fucking computer away. Instead, she leaned into his personal space and looked at him square in the face.

"You need to put this laptop away right now, not in a few minutes. We are landing on the ocean in ten minutes, and it's going to be very rough. This laptop will be a flying projectile that could take your head off. Stow it now." Her stern tone of voice meant business.

The man stopped typing, shrank in his seat, folded the laptop closed, and put it away. "Sorry."

Janine continued to help people into their life vests, and then she stowed the cabin service items. She wanted to comfort the passengers who were crying, but she didn't have time. Time seemed to be accelerating, and she didn't have time for anything. She kept seeing Molly's precious face in her mind, but she forced herself to keep working. The only way she would ever see her daughter again was if they survived this ditching and water evacuation. The lives of these passengers were in her hands, and Janine refused to allow any other thoughts to distract her.

George came to check on her. "How's it going?"

"All the life vests are on, loose items stowed, and the cabin is secure."

"Good. I'll inform Kerri that the cabin is ready. Why don't you review your evacuation commands and put on your crew life vest. Kerri will be giving us the 'Brace for impact' PA soon. You are in charge of opening door one-left after we come to a stop. I'll open door one-right. Get back to your jump seat and strap in tight."

Janine nodded. She would be responsible for opening the main cabin door after they landed on the water, making sure the slide raft inflated, and getting the passengers into the raft before the plane sank. The adrenaline buzzing through her made her hands shake.

Focus, Janine, focus. Please, God, let Kerri land this airplane safely.

❖

"Read me the ditching checklist out loud, Ray."

"We're complete except for landing preparation."

"Were you able to reach the Rescue Coordination Center for the ditching heading and sea condition?"

"No, sorry. I think we're too low. I can call Trans Global 506 again and ask them to relay our position and heading."

"Good idea. Do it now."

While Ray was calling their company aircraft, Kerri mentally visualized the procedure for landing on water. She'd practiced this maneuver exactly two times in her life in the flight simulator, so she knew what it was supposed to look like. The chances were slim, at best, that a real water landing would look like what she'd seen in the sim. The biggest difference between a water landing and a normal landing on a runway was that the landing gear would be up, instead of down. She remembered that the visual landing picture was very different with the gear up versus down. She would be setting the jet down on its belly, with the wheels up, and she would be fifteen feet closer to the water at touchdown.

Her touchdown point would be a moving target on the ocean's surface. She would have to account for the swells to land the plane. The Rescue Coordination Center was supposed to give her the wind direction at the surface, the height of the swells, and a heading to fly perpendicular to them. Kerri needed to fly this heading so the plane wouldn't get swamped by the waves and sink before everyone could evacuate.

She took a moment to look out the big windows of her 767. The sky before her was still beautiful, with bands of pink and gold near the horizon. The fluffy white clouds beneath her once again reminded her of popcorn. She loved this view more than anything in the world. When her life was in turmoil, gazing down at the earth from this high altitude put everything in perspective. Her problems never seemed so big when viewed from the sky. Today, however, all she wanted was to be able to see this view again.

Kerri had dealt with in-flight emergencies before, during her military and commercial flying careers. The situation was always tense when you had an emergency, but her training and experience had gotten her through tough ones. She'd never had to deal with real multiple emergencies and never had to land the plane on something other than a paved runway. Never, that is, until now.

"Any luck on reaching the Rescue Coordination Center?"

"Not yet, Kerri. I'll keep trying."

As they descended toward the ocean, the puffy, white clouds before her had become a solid layer. She could catch only glimpses of blue water between the gaps in the clouds. Kerri wouldn't be able to fully see the water until she'd penetrated this cloud deck, and then she'd need to quickly evaluate the sea conditions and figure out a landing heading.

"How are we coming on our checklists, Ray?"

"They're all complete except for the final landing steps."

"We don't have any altimeter setting or navigation aids for this approach, so this will be a visual single-engine landing. The radio altimeter will give us the height above the water, and I need you to call out altitudes, in hundred-foot increments, starting at five hundred feet above the water. At one hundred feet, call my sink rate. I need to touch down with zero sink just as we land. The ground proximity warning system will be disabled, since the gear will be up, so we can't rely on that."

"Okay. Got it," Ray answered, his voice shaky. Kerri needed his full attention and skill to back her up as she flew this landing.

"Ray, we're going to be all right. We just have to stay focused and work together to land this plane on the water, then get everyone out. We're passing five thousand feet, so let's get our life vests on and complete the last steps of the checklist."

Kerri reached into her seat back pocket to retrieve her orange Crew vest. She'd put it on many times during annual recurrent training, but she'd never had to wear it in the real aircraft before.

"Ray, you have the jet." She jumped up out of her seat, pulled on her dark-blue jacket with the four gold stripes on the sleeves, and grabbed her round captain's hat.

She handed Ray his hat. "Keep your hat with you and wear it in the raft. Did you bring your uniform jacket?"

"No, I didn't. We're supposed to be landing in Hawaii, so I don't have it with me." Kerri could hear an edge of anger in his voice. She'd spent her entire working life flying predominantly with men, and their first emotion was always anger. It didn't matter if they were afraid, confused, hurt, or uncertain; their initial response was to get mad. Kerri didn't have time to put up with that right now.

In her calmest voice, Kerri said, "Ray, I need you to hear me. Just back me up on the landing, and when we come to a stop, read the evacuation checklist. Then you'll go back to the cabin, to door one-right, and assist the passengers into the raft. Do you copy?"

"Yes. I understand." His voice sounded more normal, and he took a deep breath. Ray read the last checklist steps out loud as he accomplished each item. "Ground proximity gear switch, to override. Cabin, depressurize. Main outflow valve, fully closed. The checklist says to use flaps at thirty degrees for landing, but we're single engine. How do you want to fly this, Kerri?"

"I plan to use flaps at twenty degrees, and then right before touchdown, I'll call for flaps thirty. Call the cabin and make sure they're ready."

Ray rang the cabin, and then Kerri heard George's voice over the cockpit speaker. "We're all set."

"I need to make one last radio call before we land. You have the jet, Ray. Continue the descent to fifteen hundred feet."

"Roger. I have the aircraft."

Kerri keyed her mike button. "Trans Global 506, this is 401, emergency."

"Go ahead, 401."

"Trans Global 401 will be landing in five minutes. 506, write down the following. Position, north two-six degrees, zero one minutes, decimal one. West one-four-one degrees, zero two minutes, decimal zero. Heading two-seven zero degrees. Speed two-one-zero knots. Passing two thousand feet."

"Trans Global 401, this is 506. We copy your position. I'll pass your information on to the Rescue Coordination Center. They report no vessels in your immediate area at this time. San Francisco Radio has activated the Automated Merchant Vessel Report system to notify all the ships in the vicinity of your position. Anything else we can do for you?"

"No, 506. That's it. Thanks for your help."

"Good luck, 401."

Kerri descended into the cloud layer and looked at her flight instruments. Her attitude indicator showed wings level. Radio altitude, two thousand feet above the water. Airspeed too high. Kerri gently pulled her one remaining throttle to idle, pulled back on the yoke to slow down, and called, "Flaps, one."

She slowed to two hundred knots, still in the clouds. Kerri brought the nose of the jet up to two degrees high, set her descent rate to seven hundred feet per minute down, and checked her rudder and pitch trim. *Make this just like a normal approach. Nice and stable. Please, God, let me see the water.*

"Flaps, five. Speed, one-eighty."

Ray moved the flap lever to the correct position, then rotated the airspeed knob on the mode control panel.

"Approaching fifteen hundred feet," he said.

"Landing check. Flaps to twenty. Set target speed." Kerri looked at her wind indicator. It showed fifteen knots of wind from the west. Since she couldn't see any waves yet, she adjusted her heading to fly into the wind at a forty-five-degree angle.

Ray turned the airspeed knob and read the final checks. "Speed brake, down. Gear, up. Flaps, twenty. Standing by for final flaps."

Kerri looked down at her comm panel and pushed the PA button.

"This is the captain. Brace for impact. Brace, brace, brace."

"One thousand feet."

Come on, come on, let me see it!

Just then, the clouds thinned, and Kerri looked out her front window. "Oh, shit."

Before her were roiling waves ten feet high, foaming whitecaps, and gusting wind. She pushed the throttle up to slow her descent.

"The swells are from my left. Set heading to three-six-zero. I'm going to fly perpendicular to the swells and try to land on top of one."

The white, fluffy popcorn clouds had turned into a gray, ominous layer above her, with big waves beneath her. Kerri continued her descent and watched the waves, trying to find their pattern.

"Five hundred feet."

"Flaps to thirty. Check target speed."

"Flaps, thirty. Target speed, set. Landing check, complete. Sink rate, seven hundred down."

Kerri was stable and configured for landing. The waves looked bigger and bigger as she neared them.

Ray called out, "Four hundred, three hundred, two hundred."

A golden beam of light pierced the cloud deck, lighting up the sea. A shimmering spot of smooth water appeared before her. Kerri couldn't believe her eyes. It was her runway. She kicked in a little right rudder to align the nose of the jet with the glassy water.

"One hundred feet. Sink rate, three hundred."

"I have it. Landing." Kerri aimed her plane at the beam of gold pointing to her landing zone.

"Fifty feet. Sink rate, two hundred." Kerri brought her head up to see the entire horizon, keeping her wings level with the sea.

"Thirty feet. Sink rate, one hundred." She smoothly brought the throttle to idle and pulled back slightly on the yoke.

"Ten feet. Sink rate, zero." Kerri held her landing attitude and felt her speed bleed off. She eased her plane down gently. Holding her breath, she felt the tail section settle onto the water. Then she pulled back on the yoke as far as it would go to hold the nose up. She flew the nose down, and a wave of water washed over the cockpit windows.

"I can't believe we're in one piece. Evacuation checklist!"

CHAPTER ELEVEN

All the muscles in Janine's body tightened with apprehension. She'd strapped herself into her jump seat as securely as possible, but the agony of waiting was killing her. She'd trained for this possibility during her career as a flight attendant, but she'd never truly believed it would happen to her. And now, here she was, flying in a 767 over the middle of the Pacific Ocean, waiting for her captain to transmit the words no flight attendant ever wanted to hear.

She mentally reviewed her commands to the passengers to evacuate the aircraft. She'd practiced the evacuation procedure every year in recurrent training, and now she was waiting to do a real one. Her hands were shaking, and she had to fight against thinking about Molly. She couldn't entertain, for one second, the possibility she might never see her daughter again. She forced that thought from her mind, determined to do her job and to survive.

Janine could see down one of the aisles of the plane and looked at the faces of her passengers. The entire cabin was eerily quiet except for sounds of soft crying and praying. All these people had been happy and excited about their Hawaiian vacations only two and a half hours ago. Now, they all had to be worrying if they'd ever see their loved ones again. Janine looked at Mr. Shapiro in 3B. He had his head down, was holding his wife's hand, and rocked back and forth in his first-class seat. All his money meant nothing at this moment.

Janine jumped at the sound of the PA.

"This is the captain. Brace for impact. Brace, brace, brace."

All the other flight attendants shouted commands to the passengers: "Keep your head down. Brace for impact."

George, sitting next to her in his jump seat, reached over and held her hand. At least she was going through this with a friend. She always listened for the comforting sound of the landing gear coming down. Today, it felt very odd not to hear it. A chill ran through her like a bad omen, and she glanced out the small window inside door one-left and saw waves and whitecaps. *Crap. This landing is going to be bad.*

She braced herself in her jump seat, trying to keep her back straight, and held her head against the padded bulkhead. The tail section landed on the water first with a loud whoosh. She tensed, waiting for the plane to break apart and the cabin to fill with water. Then the nose came down and settled on the water, almost like a normal landing.

"Wow. That wasn't nearly as bad as I thought it would be," Janine said to George. They both held on, waiting for the jet to stop.

When the plane finally came to rest, Janine heard Kerri's command voice. "Release your seat belts and get out. Release your seat belts and get out now!"

Janine unfastened her jump seat harness and stood up by door one-left. The passengers were out of their seats and rushing toward her.

She put her hand up to stop them. "Stand back. Stand back," she shouted.

Janine grabbed the fixed handhold with her right hand, then slammed the red emergency handle into the up position. The big door came in, then rolled into the ceiling. As the door moved up, the gray slide raft fell out the bottom of it and unfurled, but it failed to automatically inflate.

"Oh, no." Janine grabbed the red manual override handle at the top of the slide, yanked it hard, and then the raft started to inflate with a loud hiss.

Thank God.

The sight before Janine stunned her. She couldn't see anything but water right in front of her door. The waves splashing against the bottom of the door brought her back to reality.

"Come this way. Leave everything behind. Jump into the raft. Move it, move it. Come this way." Janine shouted commands as loud as she could. She heard George and the other flight attendants also yelling their commands. The evacuation looked like chaos, but Janine was surprised at how orderly it was. Most people did as instructed, but a few men were trying to push their way to the front, past other passengers.

Janine heard George yell, "No shoving. We have room for everyone. Keep moving."

One man came up with his carry-on bag, trying to get onto the raft.

"Leave it. No bags allowed on the raft."

"But this is very important." The man was pleading.

"Give it to me, and I'll take care of it," Janine said. The man reluctantly let go of his bag and climbed into the raft. After he was on board, Janine threw his briefcase into the water, where it sank like a stone.

"My bag!" the man yelled.

"Sorry. I guess that wasn't a very good throw." Janine suppressed a small smile of evil glee.

Her raft, which held seventy people, was filling up quickly. She looked down the aisles of the plane, glad to see that most people were already off the aircraft. She would have to get into the raft herself very soon.

"Janine, help me scavenge the galley." George was furiously throwing everything usable from their galley into his raft, tossing water bottles, cans of soda, bags of snacks, and the first-aid kit as fast as he could.

Janine joined him, "Heads up, everyone." She threw water bottles, cans, alcohol minis, the silver metal coffee pots, and as many blankets as she could reach.

"George, have you seen Kerri get on a raft yet?"

"No, I haven't. Check the cockpit, Janine. It's almost time to go."

Janine ran to the flight deck. The door was open, and both pilots were already gone. "Good. Kerri must have gotten into a raft." As she left the flight deck, Janine looked down the length of the cabin and saw Kerri at the back of the plane helping an elderly person into one of the aft-cabin rafts.

Water sloshed in the aisles of the back of the plane and was moving forward. This airplane was going down fast. All the crew needed to get into rafts immediately.

Janine shouted, "Kerri, we have to go. Now."

❖

Kerri stopped what she was doing, turned to look at Janine, and their eyes locked for a moment.

She yelled back, "On my way."

After she'd landed on the water and come to a stop, she and Ray had completed the evacuation checklist. Then she'd directed Ray to go into the cabin and help people off the plane. Kerri had grabbed her essential equipment before she left the flight deck for the last time. She had her wallet, phone, navigation chart, paper flight plan, captain's hat, and her gun. She'd written down their final latitude and longitude on her flight plan. As Kerri left the flight deck, she turned to look back at the airplane she loved so much. Pain stabbed her. She felt like she was abandoning a wounded friend. That was her last look back.

Ray was already in the raft at door one-right, and Kerri needed to check the rest of the aircraft before she left. She was impressed that most of the plane was already empty. Just a few passengers remained, and they were getting into the aft slide rafts. Kerri ran down one aisle, glancing at every seat all the way to the back of the plane. Then she ran forward up the other aisle and saw something in seat 15G. It was a young girl, maybe thirteen, covered with a blanket and slouched down in her seat.

Kerri stopped and bent to talk to her. "Hey, it's time to go. We have to get off the plane now."

The girl said nothing. Kerri repeated herself, not wanting to physically drag this girl off the plane, but she would, if necessary. She tried a different tack, sitting down next to the girl and speaking softly to her.

"What's your name? I'm Kerri."

"My name is Melissa, but everyone calls me Mel."

"Mel, honey, we really need to go now."

"I can't. I'm waiting for my mom and dad."

Kerri looked around the empty cabin.

"Mel, I think your mom and dad must already be on a raft. Come with me, and let's go find them." She had to get Mel, and herself, into a raft immediately. Water was moving up the aisles from the tail section, and this aircraft would be sinking in seconds. "Please, Mel, trust me. We have to go right now. We'll find your parents. I promise."

Mel looked Kerri in the eye. "Okay." She reached for Kerri's hand and got out of her seat.

Kerri could feel the deck of the aircraft tipping toward the tail. Water was rushing in the two aft doors. "Run, Mel, run!"

They both dashed to the front of the plane. Only one raft was still attached to the aircraft, while the others were floating away.

Janine was waiting for them at door one-left. "Oh, my God. Where were you? We have to leave this minute."

They both helped Mel into the now-crowded raft, and then Janine climbed in, and finally Kerri. She pulled the flap at the door sill to release the raft from the plane, and they started to float away, but then the raft abruptly stopped.

"Crap. The mooring line didn't release." Kerri bent over the side of the raft, furiously feeling around for something. "Got it."

She pulled out an orange knife with a curved blade from a pocket in the raft, reached into the water, and cut the line holding them to the plane. The end of the raft snapped down from the door sill just as the nose of the plane started to rise.

"Everyone, paddle away from the plane as fast as you can," Kerri shouted. The nose rose from the water as the tail was sinking. The jet was going down, and they had to get away from it before they all got sucked under. Passengers on both sides of the raft were flinging their arms into the water and paddling like hell. They were making progress and floating away from the aircraft.

When it looked like they were a safe distance away, Kerri said, "Stop paddling."

Everyone in the raft stopped and turned to look back at their sinking jet. The tail section went down first, followed by the fuselage. The wings went next, with the nose section and cockpit last. A groaning noise came from the plane when the last air escaped from the two forward doors, as if it were a dying breath.

Kerri's heart broke as the final remnants of her magnificent 767 sank beneath the swirling waters. It was like watching her best friend slowly drown and being helpless to save her. Tears welled in her eyes, but she forced them down. She couldn't cry in front of her passengers. This raft, with seventy frightened people in it, was her vessel now, and she had to be their captain. *Oh, my God. What have I done? I'm so sorry, my old friend.*

❖

The passengers were strangely quiet after watching the plane sink. Seeing their aircraft vanish into the ocean brought the reality of their situation into sharp focus. They were all crammed into a life raft surrounded by nothing but water. And that raft was heaving up and down in ten-foot swells.

All eyes were on Kerri and Janine, and the sounds of crying

and wailing increased. These people were about to panic, and Kerri and Janine had to get them under control.

Kerri shouted loud enough to be heard over the noise of the wind and waves. "Listen up, people. We need to get this raft organized."

The passengers looked at Kerri like she was speaking Arabic.

"Here, Kerri. Let me try." Janine climbed over several passengers to get next to Kerri, holding the red megaphone she'd taken off the plane.

She spoke into it. "Ladies and gentlemen, I'm your flight attendant, Janine. Captain Kerri and I are here to keep you all safe until we are rescued." The sounds of crying seemed to decrease, the passengers listening to Janine's calming voice.

"Captain Kerri and I have extensive training on the use of emergency equipment in this raft, and on rescue procedures. It's very important that we all follow her instructions, remain calm, and work together. We will get through this. I promise."

As the passengers listened to Janine, their sense of panic seemed to subside. She handed the megaphone to Kerri. "Let's try that again."

"Thanks, Janine. You're very good with them." Kerri took the megaphone from Janine's shaking hands.

"First, we need to get the water out of the raft. You people in the middle, you're at the lowest point of the raft, and we're going to use the metal coffee pots as bailing buckets." Two male passengers in the middle started filling the coffee pots and heaving the water overboard.

"Kerri, we need to round up all the emergency equipment."

"Yes, of course." Kerri's face had an uncharacteristic hard edge. Her brow was furrowed and her full lips stretched in a thin, tight line. She appeared very stressed.

Janine reached over and lightly touched the back of Kerri's hand, and the look of fierce concentration faded.

"We have to make them believe we know what we're doing and that we're not afraid, or we'll lose them."

"You're right. Sorry. I guess I'm better with machines than I am with people. Why don't you talk to them?" Kerri handed the megaphone back to Janine.

"Please look around where you're sitting. We need to gather all the emergency supplies in this raft and pass them forward." Janine had to speak loudly even with the megaphone, to be heard over the howling wind. The seas were growing rougher by the minute.

The passengers handed the yellow survival kit to Kerri, then the raft patch kit, the backup air pump, the flashlights, the medical kit, and the emergency-locator transmitter. Janine saw a flash of yellow as Mr. Shapiro tossed something overboard.

"Mr. Shapiro, what was that?" Janine asked.

"It's nothing. Just an empty bag," he answered with an irritated expression.

Janine turned to Kerri. "I think he just threw away the sea anchor."

"God damn it." She took the megaphone from Janine.

"Ladies and gentlemen, do not throw anything overboard. We need everything on this raft in order to survive." Kerri's voice clearly expressed anger at this man's mistake.

Kerri turned to her and bent down to whisper in her ear. "We're really screwed. That idiot just threw away a vital piece of equipment. Without the sea anchor to help us hold position, we're going to drift away from the other rafts."

Janine looked across the water for the rafts from her plane. Three rafts clustered near each other in a group, but the wind and the sea were pulling their raft away from everyone else.

"Oh, no," she muttered.

They were truly on their own.

CHAPTER TWELVE

After watching the other rafts drift away from them, the passengers grew subdued and quiet. The raft listed to the right. Too many people were sitting on the right side, and the raft was unbalanced. The waves were getting bigger, and the wind picked up. They had to rearrange the passengers to stabilize their raft. Janine took her high heels off so she wouldn't puncture the raft, then maneuvered to the center of the raft to persuade people to move.

"Everyone, please take off anything sharp. Remove jewelry, shoes, large watches, pens, or anything else that could puncture our raft."

Janine made a point of looking into the faces of her passengers as she moved among them. When she asked them to shift position, she touched each person's shoulder or arm to connect with them. She smiled and thanked them for their cooperation.

Kerri was impressed with Janine's ability to lead the passengers, calm them, and get the job done. She directed them with kindness and self-confidence.

Kerri snorted out a little laugh. Who wouldn't want to follow a Nordic goddess and do everything she asked?

"What are you smiling about?" Janine plopped down next to her.

"Oh, nothing. I'm just very impressed with your ability to handle the passengers. You're very skilled."

"I'm nothing special. I just really care about them and want to take care of them."

"Well, you're doing a great job, and I appreciate it."

"Thanks, but you have to listen to me. You're coming on way too strong for these people. If you yell at them and order them around, they'll revolt."

"I don't care if they do. We're in a survival situation, and I'm not going to sweet-talk anyone."

"Kerri, you and I need these people. We can't put up the canopy by ourselves, especially in this weather. Look behind you. We're getting pulled into some very rough weather."

Kerri turned in her seat in the front of the raft, looked to the horizon, and could no longer see any sign of their other three rafts. The wind and the current had moved them far to the north of everyone else. She'd been doing mental calculations using her button magnetic compass and her favorite silver pilot's watch. Assuming they were drifting at fifteen knots, she guessed they were at least seventy-five miles off course.

Now they were drifting toward the edges of a big storm. "This isn't good."

Janine leaned into Kerri's ear. "What's not good?"

"This storm. It's the edges of a typhoon. We were well south of it on our flight's planned route, but now we're drifting right into it. We've got to secure this raft." Kerri grabbed the megaphone.

"Ladies and gentlemen, those of you near the edge of the raft, look around and you'll see a big fabric piece rolled up. We need to open it. It's the protective canopy for the raft, which will keep the rain out. We're in for some rough weather, and we need to attach this canopy to the inflated posts around the raft. Let's move quickly, please." Kerri was trying to sound calm, because they were in for a world of hurt if they didn't cover their raft.

Everyone around the perimeter of the raft busily opened the canopy and secured it to the raft posts. They had to move fast or risk having water from the waves and the rain swamp them.

"Kerri, we have to secure everything loose in the raft before this storm hits us."

Kerri picked up the megaphone again.

"Ladies and gentlemen, please look around you for anything loose and pass it forward. We need the emergency equipment, water bottles, soda cans, and any other food." Everyone was helping, and Kerri had to admit that Janine's style of speaking to the passengers was certainly better than her own. Only one person, Mr. Shapiro from 3B, wasn't joining in.

Janine crawled over some people to speak to him. Kerri was sure she could work her magic on him and get him to cooperate, until she heard him shouting at Janine.

"Get the hell away from me. I'm not putting that raft cover over my head because I'll get seasick." Then he shoved Janine backward, and she fell over some of the other passengers.

Kerri saw red when he put his hands on Janine. She jumped over other passengers to speak directly to him.

"What the hell's wrong with you? She's trying to help keep you from drowning. Put the canopy up now." She abandoned her "nice" voice and used her command voice on him.

"No, I won't. And you know what else, Captain? Fuck you. You got us into this mess, and I intend to sue you and your crappy airline. This is all your fault."

Kerri tried one last time to get through to him. "Mr. Shapiro, if we don't secure the canopy around the entire raft, we'll take on water. You're putting everyone on this raft at risk. Attach the canopy now."

"Hell, no. If you weren't so incompetent as a pilot, we wouldn't be in this situation in the first place."

Kerri grabbed the man's two-hundred-dollar necktie, pulled his face into her own, unsnapped her holster, drew her weapon, and jammed the barrel of her forty-caliber pistol into his neck. She yanked him up, shoved his head and shoulders over the side of the raft, bent over him from above, and said, "Listen up, you asshole. You are endangering the lives of every person on this raft. Either connect the canopy where you're sitting and shut the hell up, or I'll throw you overboard."

"You wouldn't dare. I'm a Million Mile Flier with your airline."

"Just watch me." Kerri pushed her gun farther into his neck.

A soft hand touched her shoulder.

"Kerri, please let him go. I'm sure Mr. Shapiro understands how important it is to safeguard our raft, and he's going to work with us now, aren't you, Mr. Shapiro?"

He appeared terrified, with Kerri's face next to his and her gun pressed next to his head.

"Ye…yes, I will. Sorry for the misunderstanding." He looked like he was about to cry.

Kerri reluctantly let go of his necktie, and he slid back down into his seat. Janine came over and attached the last part of the raft canopy to the post, just as the rain from the storm started to pelt them. Kerri holstered her weapon and returned to her seat at the front of the raft, all the passengers staring at her.

She had never pointed her gun at a real person before, only paper targets. She was still fuming about what a jerk this guy was. When he'd laid hands on Janine earlier, she'd wanted to blow his head off and see a satisfying cloud of red mist where his brain used to be. The stress of this emergency was getting to her, and maybe she'd gone too far. When Shapiro had called her incompetent and blamed her for the emergency they were in, his words had struck close to home. Had she screwed something up? Was this all her fault?

Janine came and sat next to her. "Kerri, please put your gun away. We don't need it, and now the passengers are afraid of you."

"I guess I overreacted." The rain from the storm hit them in sheets of water. The raft pitched and rolled in the giant swells. Could this get any worse?

❖

Janine's heart was pounding, and she had trouble catching her breath. In addition to being in a raft with seventy people and getting tossed around in a storm, now she had a trigger-happy captain to deal with. The passengers had just started to settle down when Kerri drew her gun on Mr. Shapiro for refusing to follow commands. True, he was a total selfish jerk, but he didn't deserve a gun pointed at his head. The expression on Kerri's face when she had him by the neck, pointing her gun at him, was frighteningly familiar.

It reminded her of the bad years of her life before Molly changed everything. Janine looked at her watch. She would normally be in her hotel room by now, changed out of her uniform dress and heels, lying on the bed, and calling her daughter. She loved hearing about Molly's day at school and the funny, quirky way she saw the world. Janine would sell her soul just to hear Molly's voice again.

The wind and high waves pushed their raft around. This storm was going to be bad and probably last all night. Janine reached for the megaphone.

"Those of you near the sides of the raft, grab onto the rope around the top of the raft. If you're sitting in the middle area, hook your arms together and hold on to each other. This is going to be a rough ride, so we all have to hang on tight."

The wind howled, and the raft rolled through the rising swells. Janine heard passengers wailing and retching but was helpless to assist them. She had her arm looped around the raft rope, hanging on as hard as she could. She'd never been seasick before, but the violent heaving made her struggle not to vomit. This torture was endless.

Kerri shouted so Janine could hear her. "Is it okay if I put my jacket around you? You're getting soaked."

"Yes. But don't take it off. Just put your arm over my shoulder. Then we both might not get too wet."

"Fat chance of that." Kerri moved close to her, opened her captain's jacket, and draped her arm and jacket over Janine's shoulders. *She feels so nice and toasty.*

"Thank you, Kerri. Sorry I'm shivering." Kerri gently pulled her into her side.

She lost all sense of time. The storm assaulted them for hours. They were in pitch darkness. She was cold and wet from the stinging sea spray, her arms ached from clinging to the rope, and the raft was still violently tossing on the frothing ocean. Was this the way Death would take her? Drown her in the middle of the ocean, her body never to be found?

Janine tried, and failed, to conjure the image of Molly's beautiful, freckled face. The only way she could withstand the pain of the rope rubbing her skin raw, and the fear that made her entire body shake, was to speak her mantra. "Hang on. Hang on, for Molly." Hour after endless hour, Janine felt her mind and her battered body sink into a pit of despair. *I'm never going to see her again.*

❖

Thursday, May 8

Kerri's eyelids were crusted closed with salt. Her right arm and hand were numb. She was nauseous and disoriented. She forced her eyes open and carefully raised the edge of the canopy to look outside. Kerri thought she was seeing an illusion. As she blinked, the vision became real. It was a thin band of dark blue against the black sky. Recognition from years of all-night flights brought a tiny smile to her cracked lips. It was the first light of dawn. By some miracle, they were still alive.

They had survived the worst night of her life. She hoped no one was seriously injured, since all they had was a first-aid kit.

The howling wind had died down, and she could hear people moaning. The raft appeared to be mainly intact, and she didn't want to wake any passengers. She took a moment to enjoy the sight of the horizon and relish the dawn light creeping into the sky. She hadn't been sure she'd ever see this sight again. It was a new day, and it certainly couldn't be any worse than yesterday.

Kerri's shoulder hurt, and she was aware of her arm still wrapped around the rope. She also felt Janine stir next to her. She had her left arm around Janine's shoulder, and both her legs were wrapped around Janine's waist. Kerri's shoulder throbbed, but she didn't want to disturb Janine. Her nearness was comforting. After enduring the Seventh Circle of Hell last night, she just wanted to enjoy the sensation of Janine next to her for a moment.

"Are we dead?" Janine's voice was raspy.

"Not yet, but we came real close. Are you all right?"

"You held on to to me with your legs. I guess I couldn't grip the rope anymore. Thanks."

Kerri disentangled herself from Janine. "We need to assess the condition of the raft and the passengers."

"Can we just take a minute to breathe and leave the raft and the passengers alone for the moment?"

"Sure."

Kerri put her logical, analytical, task-oriented brain on hold, took a deep breath, and just sat next to Janine. They were cramped and uncomfortable, but Kerri enjoyed the sensation of having Janine next to her. Her clothes were damp, her blond hair disheveled, but she was still beautiful, except for the dark circles under her eyes. They didn't speak. Instead, they just watched the eastern sky as the first light of day chased away the frightening darkness.

Watching the sun rise, after flying all night long, was one of the most beautiful sights Kerri enjoyed from her pilot's seat. The pale colors slowly emerged from the black sky—first as dark blue, then lighter blue, then soft gold and pink as the day became alive. It would be several minutes before the actual sun came up, but seeing the amazing colors of dawn gave Kerri a small glimmer of hope that they might be rescued.

"It's so beautiful," Janine whispered, like she didn't want to break the magic spell.

"Yes, it is."

They sat next to each other in silence, looking at the sky, just breathing fresh air.

Gradually they heard some of the passengers stirring as the sky grew lighter. Then the complaining started. Their moment of quiet beauty was over, and they had to deal with the reality of their situation.

Kerri looked over the side of the raft to the sea. The torrential rain had stopped, the high winds had died down, and the swells were now only five feet high. The raft was still undulating with the sea, but not as violently.

"I think it's safe to roll up the sides of the canopy and let in some air."

"I agree."

Kerri and Janine unhooked their side of the canopy, leaving it connected at the top posts. The passengers around the raft also rolled up their sides. The rush of clean air blew away the stench in the raft. Seeing the sun come up, and opening the sides of the canopy to let in the air, made the passengers calmer, the view stunning them all into silence. The rippling swells glittered with sunlight as fluffy white clouds drifted by against a pale-blue sky. It looked like a tropical postcard, except no island was present, or any land at all. The sight was both magnificent and desolate.

Janine picked up the megaphone. "Good morning, ladies and gentlemen. Congratulations on surviving the worst night I've ever had. I don't know about you, but I'll never be staying at this establishment again."

Kerri couldn't help but chuckle. They all looked like drowned rats and smelled like the floor of a dive bar, but Janine found a way to make them laugh. This girl had skills.

"Look around you for anything loose—water bottles, cans, raft equipment, food—and pass it forward to Captain Kerri. Please find the silver coffee pots, and let's start bailing out our raft."

The passengers obediently complied, and Kerri assessed their supplies. They had only three big water bottles, eight cans of Coke, two sleeves of biscotti cookies, and an entire tray of miniature liqueurs. Well, at least she could have a shot of Kahlua after this ordeal ended.

Fortunately, they still had their medical kit, raft survival kit, air pump, and raft patches, but the most critical thing was missing.

"Crap." Kerri started frantically looking all around her.

"What's the matter?"

"We're missing the emergency-locator transmitter."

Kerri grabbed the megaphone. "Folks, we need you all to look around where you're sitting. We need to find the ELT. It's bright yellow, about the size of a coffee can, and has a blue rope attached to it."

Their situation was still very dangerous, and she absolutely had to have that ELT. It was a water-activated automatic beacon that transmitted their position through the satellite GPS system to the Rescue Coordination Center. It was the homing beacon ships and aircraft used to search for them. Losing their ELT made it much more difficult for any rescue ships to find them. Their situation had just become ten times worse.

Kerri needed to inform the passengers about their very limited supply of water and food, but she kept their ELT problem to herself. She wanted to be truthful but not alarm them. She picked up the megaphone.

"Ladies and gentlemen, first, I want to thank you for helping clean out the raft. Secondly, I want to tell you about our supplies. I know many of you are still seasick, but we have very little water and food on board. I'm going to pass around one water bottle.

Every person can have a small drink of water, one ounce only, please. I'll also pass out one sleeve of cookies, and each person gets exactly one. We appreciate your cooperation."

"Captain Kerri, I don't feel good." It was Mel, the young girl from seat 15G.

"What's the matter, Mel?"

"I threw up four times last night, and my stomach still hurts."

"I'm so sorry you feel bad. We don't have very much right now, but I'm going to give you a can of Coke. Drink this slowly."

Mel took the can, sat next to Kerri, and sipped her drink. "Do you know if my mom and dad got onto one of the other rafts? They're not on this one. I checked already."

Kerri and Janine looked at each other, trying to come up with an answer. They had no idea where her parents were, or if they were even alive.

"I'm sure they're on one of the other rafts. We'll all see each other again after we get rescued." Kerri tried to sound reassuring.

"Captain Kerri, I think the ELT you asked about got washed overboard last night."

"Did you see it, honey?"

"No, but I saw a blue rope attached to the raft, floating in the water, with nothing on the end of it."

"Damn it," Kerri muttered.

"Hey, Captain. Speaking of rescue, when are you going to get us out of this disgusting raft?" It was Mr. Shapiro yelling at her from the middle of the raft, where everyone could hear him.

Kerri wanted to tell him to shut the hell up. Instead, in her most even tone of voice, she answered him.

"We gave the coordinates of our position to another aircraft, and they alerted the Rescue Coordination Center, which notifies all ships in our vicinity. I'm sure ships are headed our way as we speak."

Kerri really hoped what she'd just said was true, but she had no idea if it was. The storm last night had blown them far away from her last reported position. Without their ELT, the aircraft and ships looking for them could be hundreds of miles away searching in the wrong area. She had no clue if rescue ships were enroute or if they'd ever be found. But she had to keep this information to herself.

Just then, Kerri saw Mr. Shapiro look around quickly, presumably to make sure no one saw him. Then he pulled out a hidden full bottle of water and took a long swig.

"Hey! Where'd you get that water bottle. Pass it forward."

"I brought it with me. It's mine," he lied.

Kerri started to jump up to go take the water away from him, but Janine's hand on her arm stopped her. "Wait, Kerri. Let me talk to him first."

Janine crawled over the passengers to reach him and bent down to speak to him privately. After that, he handed his water bottle to her. She smiled at him, then returned to her seat with the water. Kerri was again impressed with her skill at handling difficult passengers.

After she sat down, Janine leaned in toward Kerri. "Is there any chance they really do know where we are after that storm?"

For a long moment, Kerri didn't answer her, but finally she whispered her reply so the passengers couldn't hear her. "I have no idea. We've been blown far away from our original position and the other rafts, thanks to that idiot throwing away our sea anchor. Worst of all, we've lost the ELT."

Janine sat in stunned silence.

"All we can do is go through our procedures and hope someone picks up our signals."

Kerri saw tears well up in Janine's eyes. She reached for her hand. "Please, Janine. We have to keep it together for the passengers."

"Okay," she answered softly.

Kerri wanted to hold Janine and comfort her. Janine was strong, smart, and very capable, but she was clearly upset. She wanted to talk to Janine, but now wasn't the time.

They had a job to do. They had to figure out how to be found.

CHAPTER THIRTEEN

Janine was fighting as hard as she could not to scream out in agony. Without their ELT, their chances of rescue had just gone from bad to way worse. She'd checked all the emergency equipment during her preflight inspection, including the spare ELT inside the overhead bin at row one. During the evacuation, when they were scavenging the aircraft before getting into the rafts, another flight attendant had grabbed the spare ELT. *Why didn't I grab that first, instead of the water bottles?*

Janine was on the verge of a meltdown at the thought of never seeing Molly again. *Don't go there, don't go there.* She had to pretend she had her shit together in front of the passengers, but she clearly didn't.

Kerri reached for her hand and looked at her. "Janine, someone's going to find us. It's just going to take longer."

Kerri's attempt to comfort her touched her. "Do you know how much longer? We don't have much water."

"I really have no idea. Our rescue went from hours, to days, maybe even weeks. We have to keep them calm, ration the water, and wait."

Kerri squeezed her hand. "We will be found. Just hang in there with me." She gave Janine a little smile.

"Captain Kerri, is there anything in here that will help us?" Mel dragged over the raft survival kit.

Kerri turned to Mel. "Yes, honey. There sure is. Let's open it."

Janine watched Kerri and Mel sort through the items in the kit. During annual training, all crew members practiced using the different emergency equipment. Spread out on a table in the training classroom, it looked like a lot of stuff. Seeing it now, it seemed rather skimpy. She listened to Kerri discuss each item with Mel.

"This is the day flare, and this is the night flare, because it has bumps on one end. That's so you can tell which one it is, even in the dark."

Mel was paying close attention to Kerri's every word.

"We have two small cans of water, a bag to catch rainwater, fishhooks, Band Aids, a signal mirror, and, most important, our sea-powered hand radio."

"How does it work?"

"We open this bottom part, fill it with sea water, and a chemical reaction with the salt water powers the radio for about thirty minutes. We flip this switch on the top, and then we can transmit on the emergency frequency. If any ships or planes are within range, they'll be monitoring the frequency and listening for us. Let's try it on the hour and the half hour."

Janine observed how patient and thorough Kerri was with Mel. She wasn't maternal, but more like a mentor. Maybe Kerri had taught flying in her past before she became a 767 captain. She was a good teacher. All she knew was that Mel was engaged with Kerri and not thinking about her lost parents. Mel had a band of freckles across the bridge of her nose and dimples in her cheeks. *This could be Molly in a few years.*

Fear clutched her. *What if I never see her again?* Janine had to force her thoughts to stay on the present. She couldn't allow herself to think about Molly. She had to stop looking at Mel. This young girl, all alone on the ocean, reminded her too much of her own daughter, and their similarity was tearing her up inside.

"I'm going to check on the passengers."

Janine could do her job, take care of her passengers, and wait for their rescue, no matter how long it took. She would never give up hope.

❖

"I have a very important job to do, and I need your help with it," Kerri said.

Mel answered enthusiastically. "Okay. Tell me what to do."

"Let me show you how the signal mirror works. Find the sun in the sky. We're going to flash that bright sunlight with the mirror to any passing ships or planes. Hold it up to your eye and look through the hole in the center of the mirror. You change the angle of the mirror to reflect the sun at your target."

"Like this?" Mel held the signal mirror against her right eye.

"Yes. Now aim the center circle at, say, Mr. Shapiro over there."

Mel did as instructed, and a bright, white light flashed across Shapiro's smarmy face.

"Hey, what the hell?" he snapped.

"Just testing our emergency equipment, sir." Kerri tried not to laugh at him.

"Now hit your target with three short flashes, followed by three long flashes."

Mel complied, and Shapiro yelled, "Knock it off, or I'll knock your block off!"

"Really? Go ahead and try," Kerri answered as she opened her jacket to show him her pistol.

"I'm still suing you." He snorted, then turned his back on her.

"Flash the bald spot on the back of his head, and repeat the sequence—three short, three long."

"Is that a message?"

"Yes, Mel. It's SOS in Morse code. This is your job on our raft, and it's very important to help us be seen. Take my watch, and every fifteen minutes, I want you to use the signal mirror all around the horizon for ships, and back and forth across the sky for planes. Can you do that?"

"Yes, I can, Captain Kerri."

"Good. I'm going to appoint you my captain's assistant on this raft."

Mel smiled for the first time, then got busy with her signaling duties.

Kerri looked for Janine across the raft. She was attending to passengers with small injuries and giving sips of Coke to the worst seasick cases. She was so kind to everyone that it surprised her when Janine was rather cold to Mel. She barely looked at the girl and wouldn't speak to her. This didn't add up to what she knew about Janine. What was the issue between them? If she was honest with herself, she wanted to know everything about Janine.

Despite all that had happened, Kerri was still attracted to, and intrigued by, Janine Case. Maybe after they got rescued, Kerri could ask her out on a proper date. *If* they got rescued.

Kerri poked her head out from under the canopy to look at the entire sky. She always looked at the sky, even when she was at home. Kerri loved looking at clouds. She wasn't just assessing the weather; she had to see the clouds against the blue sky. No matter how bad her day was, if she was able to look at the sky, it was a good day. That's why she chose her home in an LA high-rise, so she could view the sky every day and wake up to it.

Now, however, she studied the sky in light of their survival situation. The usually shimmering blue ocean of this morning was steel gray. The white, puffy clouds had become a broken cloud layer about three thousand feet above them. This cloud deck would make them almost invisible to search aircraft.

Kerri watched the cloud deck accelerate as it moved across the sky. This movement indicated the wind was picking up and they could be in the path of more bad weather from the typhoon. The swirling wind could even pull them farther into the eye of the storm. If that happened, they would never survive.

Kerri realized she had no control whatsoever over her fate, a very uncomfortable feeling. She prided herself on her calm, cool demeanor when flying as a captain. She never raised her voice, never panicked, never lost control. She also never lost control of any other aspect of her life. She was methodical, organized, competent, and self-assured in everything she did. Everything, that is, until she had to land her jet on the ocean, abandon it, and end up in this raft.

She was responsible for the lives of all these people, a privilege she'd earned by her skill and leadership, and she always honored it. Her passengers trusted her with their lives every time they walked onto her jet. Now, she could do very little to save them. She made her "Mayday" radio calls every thirty minutes, knowing only a slim chance existed that anyone would hear them because they were so far off their original route.

Kerri couldn't believe that her life could end in this raft, with these people. She'd had such great plans for her layover in Kona with Janine. She'd made a reservation at her favorite restaurant on the Big Island, with a gorgeous view of the sunset over the ocean. From there they could watch sailboats, outrigger canoes, and surfers as the waves broke against the sea wall next to their table. It was the most romantic place Kerri could think of to have dinner with Janine.

Kerri had planned to invite Janine to walk with her along the beach after dinner, to the best Hawaiian shave-ice place on the island. Then she would walk Janine back to her hotel room and hope Janine would invite her in. There they would kiss good night. A wave splashed cold water into her face and washed the fantasy about Janine from her mind. She wiped the salty water off her face with her sleeve. *What an idiot I've been.*

The day seemed to drag on forever. Even though the water was cold, the air temperature was warm, and people were sweating. The passengers were quiet and listless, many of them probably dehydrated. She and Mel kept signaling, hour after hour, even though the clouds were now a solid layer obscuring the sky. The wind picked up, and the increasing swells made the raft pitch and roll again. Kerri evaluated the weather.

The clouds, horizon, and sea were indistinguishable from each other in a gray mist. The wind whipped up the water into whitecaps. Lightning bolts struck the water from a line of clouds in the distance. They were drifting right toward the lightning. Another horrible night in the raft loomed. They might make it, or this would be her last night on earth. Either way, they were at the mercy of the sea.

❖

After several hours of mind-numbing boredom, Janine sat by herself, turned away from the passengers, and stared at the ocean. She'd always loved living near water. Whether it was the beach in San Diego, Lake Michigan, or even the Mississippi Gulf Coast, during the time her dad was stationed at Keesler Air Force Base, she was drawn to water. The endless ocean that she'd loved as a child was now trying to kill her, and she had very little way to defend herself. She was starving, thirsty, nauseous, exhausted, and angry.

Janine was very angry. It was the old anger, the old bad anger. The rage, like molten lava just beneath her surface, was accelerating. Her nerves were frayed. She was descending into a familiar dark place and could do nothing to stop herself. The maw of the pit of despair called to her again. This was the same pit she'd fought against to reclaim her life. In the past, Janine had been able to muster her last fragment of hope to claw her way out of that horrible place. That hope had come from Molly.

The dark pit before her now was the ocean. The same feelings of helplessness and desperation gripped her throat, making it hard to swallow. Bobbing up and down on the water, she once again had no control over life. She was losing her battle to resist the overwhelming panic. The only thing left to do was to curl up in a ball and wait for the relief of death.

❖

Kerri looked for Janine but couldn't find her. *How can you lose someone on a raft surrounded by water?* She glimpsed something blue on the far side of the raft under a blanket and climbed over the people in the raft to reach it.

"Hey. Are you okay?"

Janine didn't answer.

"Janine? Can you talk to me?" Kerri was growing very concerned.

"Leave me alone," Janine mumbled.

"Are you hurt? I can't leave you alone. We are the crew of this raft, and we have a job to do."

"What job? Do you actually think we can do anything to help us be rescued? We've done all we can, Kerri. I've just accepted the fact that we won't make it. I suggest you do the same."

Kerri had no response. Janine was always so confident and friendly, but this change in her attitude alarmed her. It looked like Janine was giving up, and Kerri had to figure out how to reengage her. She needed her, now more than ever, with another night of fierce weather looming before them.

Kerri squeezed in next to her. She needed to talk to her, but she didn't want any of the passengers to overhear them.

Kerri leaned in close. "What's going on with you? Can I do anything to help?"

"No. Nothing. Please, Kerri, just let me be."

Kerri sat in silence, struggling for words to break through to Janine. They were all suffering from dehydration, lack of food, and illness, but she and Janine had been trained to survive, and Kerri expected more from her. Maybe Janine wasn't as strong as she appeared. They were in a life-threatening situation, and she'd never heard of anyone actually surviving ditching an aircraft in the ocean, but she didn't understand why Janine suddenly appeared to have given up.

"Janine, please talk to me. I'm worried about you."

"I can't. I'm sorry."

Just then, Mr. Shapiro shouted at them. "Hey, you two. We need water over here right now."

Kerri felt the urge to reach for her gun again, but she saw Janine flinch when he yelled at them.

"Did he say something to you? Did he hurt you? If he did, I'll throw him overboard. I've had enough crap from this entitled ass." She started to get up, but Janine reached out to stop her.

"No, Kerri. He didn't hurt me. It's not him."

"Not him? I don't understand. Did someone else hurt you?"

Janine didn't answer but curled herself into a tighter ball.

"Please tell me what happened. I want to help, if I can."

"It doesn't matter. We're not going to make it, are we?"

Kerri whispered, "Don't say that. I believe someone will find us. I just don't know when, or how long it will take."

"We're not going to survive another night in a typhoon. Even I know that, and we're being blown into it."

Kerri turned away from Janine. She couldn't look her in the face. Janine's words settled on her heart like a cold stone. They were adrift in a small raft on the vast ocean. She looked at the gray horizon and saw their fate before them as lightning lit up the clouds. Janine was right. They weren't going to make it.

CHAPTER FOURTEEN

It was clear Kerri didn't want to talk to her anymore. Talking was pointless anyway, with their inescapable doom in front of them. She'd always hoped for a quick death, especially when she was in his hands. She'd prayed for him to kill her, but God always abandoned her, just like now. Maybe it was her destiny, or karma, to suffer at the end, to pay for her many transgressions.

Janine had accepted her own death many years ago, when her life had turned to darkness, after meeting Ryan Jackson.

"We don't have to say anything. Is it okay if I just sit with you?" Kerri asked.

"Sure. You're the captain."

"I'm sorry. I am so very, very sorry." Kerri's voiced cracked.

"Sorry about what? We had a huge emergency over the ocean. Several emergencies, as I recall. You landed the plane on the water. We did a kick-ass evacuation and ditching, and we all got out. We just got separated from everyone else. Kerri, you and I both know we had very little chance of survival. We did okay, considering the crappy hand we were dealt."

"You're right. We did an okay job, and thanks, I think. That was a compliment, wasn't it?"

"Yeah, it was. You made a smooth landing in a 767 on the ocean. It was amazing. I wish we could've had a chance to fly together again."

"Really? I thought you wanted nothing to do with me."

"No. That's not true. I really enjoyed our layover in Maui and the night flight back to LA."

Kerri looked confused. "Then why didn't you answer any of my calls or texts?"

Janine sighed. "It's a long, boring story."

"I'm not going anywhere right now, and I'm interested." Kerri sounded sincere.

"I didn't return your calls because I can't be in a relationship with anyone."

"I wasn't asking for a relationship. I just wanted to take you out to dinner."

"I felt sparks, Kerri, and I know you did too."

Kerri looked down for a moment before answering. "Yes. I felt a connection with you too. That's why I was so persistent. Why can't you be in a relationship with anyone? Are you married?"

Janine couldn't put the words together to explain her past. She had no explanation, no excuse, for what she'd done. What Ryan had forced her to do. She couldn't let the last words she'd ever speak be about that monster.

"Yes. I'm married."

❖

Kerri asked no further questions of Janine.

She was rarely surprised by things people did, but she'd never expected Janine to be married. She just didn't seem to be the type of person who would cheat on her husband with another woman. But then again, she'd been fooled by other women, and getting involved with a married lady always seemed to get her in trouble.

She'd thought things were different with Janine. More than anything, when Kerri had first met her, she'd seemed to be an honest, kind person. She remembered Janine's apprehension when they first went snorkeling in Maui, and then the way she overcame her fear and finally trusted Kerri in the water.

Where had that woman gone? Why was she now a curled-up ball of hopelessness? True, they were in a desperate situation, but what had made this bright, beautiful woman turn into a sullen, angry mess? Since it was Kerri's last few hours of life, she had to know.

"So, if you're married, why did you kiss me on the flight deck?"

"You kissed me, as I recall." Janine poked her head out from under her blanket.

"Okay, let's say it was a mutual decision, so why?"

"Why not? You're a gorgeous woman, it was very romantic that night, and I wanted to kiss you. That's all."

Kerri didn't believe her. "So, I was just a bi-curious bit of fun?"

"No. You certainly were not."

Kerri was becoming more confused. "Are you married to a woman?"

Janine sighed. "No. I'm not married to a woman."

"Then what gives, Janine? I really would like to understand."

Janine sat up, pulled her head out from under her blanket, and turned to face Kerri.

"As I said, it's a long, boring story. Since we'll be dead soon, what's the point of hiding it anymore? Yes, I'm married to a man, Ryan Jackson, but we've been separated for three years. I intended to divorce him as soon as I could save the money for a high-powered attorney."

"Why do you need a high-priced divorce lawyer? Is he being difficult?"

"Difficult doesn't come close to describing this man. Ryan is wealthy, powerful, and vindictive, and we have a five-year-old daughter."

"Oh, I see."

"No, Kerri. You don't see." Janine pulled up the long sleeve of her uniform dress to reveal a dozen raised circles on the inside of her upper arm. "These are from Ryan. He would burn me with his cigarettes when I didn't do what he told me to."

Kerri looked at the scars on her flawless skin with horror. What kind of bastard would do this to his wife?

"Did you know he was like that when you married him?"

"Of course not." Janine hesitated, like she was struggling whether to say any more.

"You don't have to talk about this if you don't want to." Kerri needed more information, but she didn't intend to pry.

"At this point, it doesn't matter if I try to hide it anymore. I want you to know why I couldn't call you back. My daughter and I are on the run. My husband is violent and abusive, and I have to maintain a very low profile to keep us safe from him."

Kerri tried not to react, just listen.

"I met Ryan in college. He was a handsome, fun frat boy with money. I knew I liked women, but I got drunk at a party and woke up with him on top of me. He was very charming, and he convinced me to date him, and then I ended up pregnant. He wanted me to get rid of the baby, and I sure didn't want one, but I just couldn't go through with an abortion. He was mad at me, but he said we had to get married because I was carrying the next heir to the family fortune."

"Wow. Did you want to marry him?"

"No, but I didn't know what to do. Then his family worked on me. He took me to meet them, and his parents were nice, living in a huge mansion. They were thrilled we were having a baby and promised I'd never have to worry about anything. They insisted on paying for everything, but they wanted a quick, small wedding, with no press. I felt like I was caught in a big machine, had no say in anything, and was just dragged along."

"Did you love him, Janine?"

"Not really. I thought I could learn to love him, for the sake of the baby, but I was wrong. Also, my own parents were furious with me for getting pregnant. My dad told me I was a stupid loser and was throwing my life away. They cut me off financially, and they didn't even want to meet Ryan."

"I'm sorry they reacted that way. That must have been very hard for you."

"They were right, and I was an idiot to marry him, but I did it anyway. In the beginning, he got used to the idea of having a baby and was good to me. He bought only the best of everything and became obsessed over my body as I grew bigger. Apparently, he had a thing for pregnant women. He started demanding all this weird sexual stuff. I tried to go along with it, to make him happy, but I just couldn't. That's when he started drugging me."

"He drugged you when you were pregnant? What the fuck was wrong with him?"

"Everything was wrong with him, Kerri. Absolutely everything."

Janine was silent, and then Kerri saw a tear roll down her cheek. She reached over and gently took Janine's hand in hers.

"We don't have to talk anymore." They sat next to each other on the raft, shoulder to shoulder, not speaking.

❖

Janine settled against the comfort of Kerri's shoulder, her eyes closed, fighting the demons from her past. Why had she even opened her mouth about Ryan? Was she making some futile attempt to purge all her resentment and self-loathing, like popping a giant pustule, before she died?

No. It wasn't that. It was a lot simpler than trying to purge herself. In the last moments of her life, she just wanted to be honest with someone, for the first time in many years. She wanted to tell her truth to someone who cared about her, in hopes she could forgive herself for the mess she'd made of her life.

Kerri didn't judge her but just listened with kindness on her face. She hadn't intended to tell Kerri about the abusive relationship she'd been in with Ryan. She only wanted to tell Kerri why she had to rebuff her calls and texts. But something about Kerri made her feel like she could trust her. It wasn't her captain's authority, or her dashing good looks, but some other quality that made Janine feel safe to talk to her. Maybe it was because Kerri was a person you could count on.

Whether she was piloting a massive 767, helping a novice snorkeler, or being in charge of a raft with seventy panicked people, Kerri sought out responsibility. She stepped up to be a leader when others ran away. As a flight attendant, Janine trusted her with her life when she was working in the cabin, and she trusted her now.

"What's your daughter's name?"

"Molly. She's about to turn six." Janine tried to swallow in spite of the lump in her throat.

"What does she look like?" Janine sensed Kerri's kindness as she tried to steer the conversation to a different topic.

"She kind of resembles a younger version of Mel. She has freckles, strawberry-blond hair, and the biggest smile you've ever seen. She's the light of my life."

"Is that why you ignored Mel? Because she looks like your daughter?"

"Yes, and she doesn't deserve that. I just can't face the fact that I'll never see Molly again."

Kerri reached for her hand. "I'm sure she knows how much you love her."

Janine had to change the subject, or she would be a blubbering mess. "Who's waiting for you at home?"

"Just my dog, Brownie. She's a sweet old thing, and I have a great pet sitter."

Kerri became very quiet and stared straight ahead.

Janine gave her space for a few minutes, then felt the wind whip cold salt spray against the back of her neck. Their time was very limited, and she wanted to know more about Kerri.

"Will you tell me about your family?"

"Huh? Oh, sorry. I wasn't listening."

"What's the matter, Kerri? Do you have some kind of plan?"

"I wish, but I'm all out of ideas. I was just wondering if I could have done anything differently during that emergency. Maybe I missed something on a checklist, or the fuel leak, and I could have saved the gas so we could've made it to Hilo. I'm wracking my brain."

Janine saw the genuine concern on Kerri's face.

"What's the point of beating yourself up? We are where we are. You did your best, didn't you? That's all that matters."

"It's nice of you to say that, but that's not the point. I'm responsible for all this." She swept her arm across the entire raft.

"If I made a mistake, everyone's death will be my fault." Kerri looked away from her.

Janine's heart ached at the anguished look on Kerri's face. She turned Kerri's cheek toward her. "You didn't cause this. An engine blew up. Shit happens." She looked deep into Kerri's eyes. Kerri had to hear her words.

"Guilt is a useless emotion. It doesn't solve anything, and believe me, I know. Don't waste your last hours on earth on something you cannot change."

Kerri put her hand over Janine's and held it to her face. "Thank you."

Janine looked over her shoulder at the darkening horizon. "Let's talk about something else. Why did you keep calling me after I didn't respond?"

Kerri smiled sheepishly. "Because I had a great time with you in Maui, and I couldn't stop thinking about you."

Janine's face felt hot. She knew her ears were red and hoped Kerri wouldn't notice. A vision of Molokini came into her mind, and she felt herself smile.

"Maui was so beautiful. I had a great time with you too."

"I felt something with you when we kissed on the flight deck. I know you felt it too. I was just confused that you didn't want to talk to me. I didn't know about your family situation, and I didn't mean to harass you. I'm sorry."

"It's okay. I knew it could never go anywhere because of Ryan. I didn't mean to be rude to you, despite what the Stew Network said."

"What did the Stew Network say?"

"Let's just say, they were less than complimentary."

"Now I really want to know. What did they tell you about me?" Kerri appeared very intense.

"Well, a few people said you were a womanizer with a very notched-up bedpost."

"Really. I think I can guess who told you that. Based on what they said, I can understand why you'd never want to become involved with me. Too bad you believed them."

"They said your nickname was Don Juanita. What was I supposed to think?"

Kerri chortled. "I guess I deserve that."

Janine laughed with her. Kerri's soft brown eyes sparkled when she laughed.

They leaned back against the raft tube, their hands still connected.

"You know what?"

"What's that?"

"I have many regrets in my life, but the most recent one is that I didn't return one of your phone calls. I would've liked to go on another date with you." She squeezed Kerri's hand.

Kerri returned the squeeze.

"I was planning on taking you to my favorite restaurant in Kona. You can watch the sun set into the ocean from your table."

"That sounds lovely. I'm sorry we'll never get a chance to do that." Tears stung her eyes.

What was the point of trying to maintain her composure in front of the passengers anymore? She'd never see Molly again, she and Kerri had never even had a chance, and soon her life would be over. The impending doom weighed her shoulders down like an impossible burden. At least she wouldn't face death alone.

Please, God. Make it quick.

CHAPTER FIFTEEN

Kerri sat next to Janine but had nothing to say. She was overwhelmed. Her sense of failure, and the impending death of all of them, made her feel powerless. This was a rare, and awful, emotion. She'd worked hard her entire life to excel in school, in sports, in pilot training, and even in her relationships that never seemed to work out. But now, she could do nothing to save her passengers and crew.

Kerri didn't fear many things in life. As a military combat pilot, she'd gone up against enemy aircraft and always prevailed. She'd never been afraid of dying in a plane crash because she'd always felt safe in a jet, even when dealing with an emergency. It was her destiny to fly, and she was at home in the sky. She was always confident in both her flying ability and her skill leading a crew. Now, she was waiting for her biggest threat to consume her.

Kerri had never been able to overcome her fear of drowning. She loved the beach and water sports, but she'd never even tried scuba diving because she feared suffocating under the water.

The only time she'd ever been uncomfortable in a plane was when she was flying over the North Atlantic at night in the winter. The thought of ending up in those frigid waters gave her nightmares.

For the sake of her passengers, Kerri would try to muster her final remnants of courage to face death. They had all trusted her with their lives when they boarded her 767 three days ago, and now they would all die together.

"Captain Kerri! Captain Kerri!" Mel was excitedly climbing over passengers to get to her. "Look over here."

"What is it?"

"I saw flashes. Over there." Mel pointed to the north.

"Are you sure? Was it your signal mirror reflecting on the water?"

"No, Captain Kerri. They flashed SOS back to me. Come over here and look." She grabbed Kerri's hand and pulled her up.

Mel pointed to a slight gap in the clouds. "Watch what happens." She brought the signal mirror up to her eye and flashed her dot-dash code.

"Are you seeing an airplane?"

"No. Look to the right of that gap in the clouds, at the water, and wait."

After a few seconds, Kerri saw the unmistakable three dots, three dashes flashed back at them from a spot on the northern horizon.

"Oh, my God. That might be a ship. Mel, keep signaling. Where's the emergency kit? I need the flares."

Janine had joined them on the north side of the raft. "Kerri, is there really something out there?"

"I'm not sure yet. It might be a ship."

Mel shouted, "Captain Kerri, I see something."

"Where, honey?" Kerri stood behind Mel looking in the direction she was pointing.

"Right there. I see a black speck."

"Well, I'll be damned. Mel, you're amazing. That's a ship all right, and it's headed for us."

Janine grabbed Kerri's arm. "Do you think we might actually be rescued?"

"I don't know, but we're going to do our best to make sure they see us. Just pray they reach us before we get pulled into that storm."

From the west, lightning flashed inside the towering clouds. The wind blew harder and pushed the raft toward the storm. It would be a race to see who reached them first—another violent storm or their rescue ship.

Everyone buzzed at the news of a ship coming toward them. Kerri held both their emergency flares in her hands, waiting for the ship to move a little closer before she popped her smoke. The water was moving with ten-foot swells. Even if the ship made it to them in time, it would be difficult getting seventy people off the raft and into the ship in these rough seas.

Kerri could make out the bow of the ship as it powered closer. It wasn't a huge cargo ship, but at this point, any ship would do. She climbed over to the west side of the raft so she'd be downwind when she popped her flare.

"Everyone, move back," she said.

Leaning over the side of the raft so none of the burning magnesium from the flare would touch it, she snapped the top off the flare, and a plume of bright-orange smoke rose to the sky. She had only one more flare left.

"Come on. Let me know you see us."

Kerri spotted a red arc in the sky as someone on the ship responded to her signal with their own flare.

"They see us! Everyone, wave your arms and make some noise."

The passengers frantically waved at the ship, and people started to jump up and down.

"Stay seated, stay seated. We have to keep the raft safe until they reach us."

"Kerri, is this real, or is it a mirage? Are we truly being rescued?" Janine asked.

"This ship is definitely real. We still have to control the passengers to safely get them from the raft to the ship. I need you to help me keep them organized."

Janine crawled across the raft to get passengers to help her maintain order.

The bow of the ship was rising and falling in the waves. They had all their running lights on, and Kerri could see lettering on the side of the bow. It was the USS *Sally Ride.*

A voice pierced the howling wind. It was the loudspeaker from the ship.

"This is the United States Navy. Do not attempt to exit until we secure your raft to our ship. Remain calm, and we will assist you with boarding. Stand by for further instructions."

A collective cheer rose from the passengers. Maybe their ordeal would soon be over, if the large waves didn't swamp them first.

Kerri could hardly believe her eyes. The ship looked huge compared to their raft. She still had to get everyone onto the ship, but she began to feel some relief from her burden of guilt. She watched a big crane lower a black Zodiac skiff into the water as the ship turned and slowly approached.

The ship's loudspeaker sounded again. "Remain clear of the rescue boat. Sailors will secure your raft, then tow it to the ship and help all of you get aboard safely. Do exactly what the sailors direct you to do."

The raft was heaving up and down in the water as the ship neared. Two sailors from the Zodiac tied tow ropes to the raft, then pulled them through the rough water to the ship. A platform lowered from the ship's stern.

As they approached the back of the ship, Kerri saw a figure in a blue camouflage uniform standing on the deck above the platform.

"Secure those lines to the raft. As soon as it's on the platform, get the passengers out. Get a move on. We have to leave now!"

The sailors lashed the raft to the platform with their ropes, and then other sailors ran up to the raft and lifted people out.

The commander on the deck yelled, "Make two lines. Don't push. We will get everyone on board. Move into the equipment bay as fast as you can. Is anyone injured? Corpsmen, front and center."

"Well, I'll be damned. Our rescue ship has a woman captain," Kerri said.

The name on her uniform read "Gentry," and she had short, salt-and-pepper hair. Standing with her hands on her hips, she barked commands to her crew. They quickly helped everyone off the raft and into the ship. Kerri noticed Mr. Shapiro was one of the first ones off the raft, and then he huddled in a corner, crying. To be fair, everyone was crying after they got off, including Janine. Kerri looked around to make sure everyone was off before she left.

"Come on, Captain Sullivan. It's time to go." The ship's skipper held out her hand and assisted Kerri out of their life raft.

Kerri looked into her gray eyes, climbed out, and threw her arms around her. "Thank you, thank you, thank you." She didn't even try to hold back her tears.

"We'll have time for that later, Captain. Get your passengers squared away, and my corpsmen will take care of their medical needs. I need to load your raft on board, and then we'll get the hell out of here before the storm hits."

"Why don't you just cut it loose? We don't need it anymore."

"Can't do that. I have orders to retrieve it. It's evidence." Then she turned to her sailors. "Stow the Zodiac, haul that raft in, and then secure the platform."

Her crew answered. "Aye, ma'am."

The crew struggled with the bulky mess, and then Kerri saw the skipper draw a big black knife from her belt and stab both the top and bottom raft tubes. The crew dragged it aboard as air hissed out of it.

Kerri felt a twinge of sadness seeing the gray raft deflate. *Thanks for keeping us alive, old friend.*

❖

Janine had been the next-to-last person off the raft and went to work helping the passengers get situated in the ship's bay, even directing the US Navy corpsmen to the most ill people. They were all crying and hugging each other, and she cried along with them, hardly believing they'd actually been rescued. Maybe all this was a dream and she was delirious. She kept looking over her shoulder to make sure Kerri got off the raft and finally saw her leave it and hug the ship's captain.

Janine was confused that the sailors had brought their raft on board, especially in light of the big waves. She looked around the equipment bay, with its odd-shaped, covered objects attached to the walls. It wasn't a huge space, and they filled it to capacity.

After the deflated raft was aboard, the bay doors closed, and the ship's commander stepped up onto a box so everyone could see her.

"I'm Lieutenant Commander Stacey Gentry, skipper of the US Navy Research Vessel *Sally Ride*. I wish I was welcoming you aboard under better circumstances, but we're glad you're here, and my crew will do its best to take care of all of you. I know you must be tired, hungry, and thirsty. I have only two corpsmen to attend to your medical needs, but we will get to all of you. My sailors have graciously agreed to let you use their bunks after you've received food and water. It will be very crowded on board until we get you to Honolulu, which will take several hours. This will be a rough ride until we establish some distance between us and the storm. Finally, no one is allowed on the aft fantail deck. We have classified equipment on board, so please respect that request. I have to return to the bridge, and my officer of the deck, Lieutenant Morris, will take care of any of your questions. Captain Sullivan, I need you to come with me."

Janine was impressed with this no-nonsense woman, who reminded her a little of Kerri. They weren't out of danger yet, with the storm churning up the seas, but at least they were alive and on a real ship.

More than anything, Janine needed to talk to Molly and explain why she hadn't called her. Molly was a very smart girl, and she'd know something was wrong if her mother didn't phone her as planned. Janine maneuvered across the bay to reach Lieutenant Morris.

"Sir, could you help me find a phone? I really need to call my daughter."

"I'm sorry, ma'am, but the skipper said our satellite comm is down right now due to the bad weather. I'm sure you can use our equipment as soon as the system comes back up."

Janine felt like she might scream. After the ordeal they'd been through, she needed to hear Molly's voice, and now she had to wait even longer.

"Ma'am, are you all right? You don't look too good. Have you had any water yet?"

"I'm fine, thank you. Just a little dizzy." Janine swayed, then saw a sparkly gold tinge around everything. She'd experienced this uncomfortable feeling before, when Ryan had choked her to blackout. "I just need to sit down a minute."

Lieutenant Morris ran over to Janine's side as her legs gave out, and then she was falling. She sensed strong arms grab her waist as her vision faded to black. The next thing she knew, she was lying on her back on a metal table with bright lights overhead shining in her face.

"Where am I?"

"In our sick bay, ma'am. You passed out. Please don't try to get up. The corpsman put an IV in your arm and said you're very dehydrated. Are you all right? You fought us when we tried to bring you to sick bay." Lieutenant Morris looked very concerned as he nervously patted her hand.

"Sorry about that," she said quietly. Bad memories of being choked repeatedly, then revived, flooded back to her. The familiar panic also returned as she frantically looked around the room for an escape.

"You're not on that raft anymore, ma'am. You're safe here." Lieutenant Morris gently placed his hand on her shoulder. "Please try to relax and stay here on the bed. After we get some fluids in you, you should start to feel better soon."

"All right."

Janine tried to calm her breathing. Logically, she knew she was in the sick bay of a navy ship, but her emotions betrayed her as she battled her old fear and helplessness.

This navy lieutenant was trying to be kind, but she wanted Kerri. Something about Kerri's presence made her feel calm, despite the ordeal they'd been through.

"Could you please find Captain Sullivan for me?"

"Yes, ma'am. I'll be right back." She appreciated Lieutenant Morris's willingness to help her. And she would be fine as soon as Kerri got back to her. She slid into the dark oblivion of exhaustion, thinking of holding Kerri's hand.

❖

Kerri followed Lieutenant Commander Gentry up some steep stairs to the bridge.

"Skipper on deck." All the bridge staff stood and turned to face their leader.

"Status report." Stacey Gentry's voice was clear and direct.

"Aft platform is closed, all equipment on deck is secure, recovery checklist complete. We're ready, Skipper."

"Helm, all ahead full. Make the heading one-two-zero degrees."

"But, ma'am, the standard operating procedure is slow-ahead speed with these seas."

The entire bridge went silent.

Lieutenant Commander Gentry stood quietly, her hands balled into tight fists at her hips.

"Mister Gonzalez, do you think I am unaware of the SOP speed for rough waters?"

"No, ma'am. I was just asking if—"

"All. Ahead. Full. Now." Her eyes could melt steel.

"All-ahead full. Aye, ma'am. Heading, one-one-zero, for one-two-zero. Aye, ma'am."

"Get us out of here, Mister Gonzalez."

"Aye, ma'am."

"Gunny, front and center." The skipper pointed to a huge marine.

"Captain Sullivan, you need to go with Gunnery Sergeant Blake. He'll secure your weapon for you."

"Ah, Skipper. It's not my gun, and I'm not supposed to relinquish control of it to anyone."

"I understand. The federal air marshals own your weapon, but on my ship, we have to secure all firearms. Do not fight me on this, Captain."

"Certainly not, Skipper." Kerri dutifully followed the gunnery sergeant to the weapons locker.

"Just sign here, Captain, and then you can go sit in the skipper's office. She'll be right in."

"But I need to check on my passengers and crew." Kerri was growing frustrated.

"Sorry, ma'am. The skipper was very clear. You are to wait in her office."

"I understand." Kerri knew better than to try to fight military regulations.

She had to chuckle, remembering her days in T-38 fighter lead in training. As student pilots, they got hammered if they broke a rule, mainly because the rules were in place due to previous aircraft crashes. When she was learning to be a fighter pilot, she was rewarded for her aggressiveness and for bending the rules as far as they would go without breaking. She had learned to fly her jet better than her classmates and made her aircraft do amazing things she never even thought possible. She'd also scared the crap out of herself numerous times, pushing the edge of the envelope just a little too far. She was always able to save her own ass, and her confidence grew. But all her confidence, flying skills, and years of experience meant nothing now. She was not in any position to make demands of a crew who followed their skipper into dangerous waters to rescue them. She was just a powerless stowaway.

This crew wouldn't bend any rules. Lieutenant Commander Gentry ran a tight ship, and she quashed a moment of insubordination with practiced efficiency.

Kerri sat in the skipper's office in a well-worn leather armchair. The weight of fatigue settled on her chest with a heaviness she'd never known. She fought to keep her eyes open, but she was going under the water in the raft again. Fear gripped her throat. *What does she mean by "evidence"?*

Kerri sensed warmth by her left shoulder and heard mumblings that might be words. She tried to focus, but her eyes wouldn't open.

"Kerri. Kerri, wake up." It was Stacey Gentry's voice.

Kerri sat up abruptly, gasping for air.

"Hey, hey, you're okay. You're on my ship." Stacey sat on the arm of the chair with her arm around Kerri's heaving shoulders.

Where am I? What time is it? What day is it?

Kerri abhorred waking up disoriented in a strange room, or in some foreign city, not knowing where she was or what time it was. It was an occupational hazard for airline pilots, who forced themselves to stay awake all night flying across the country or crossed eight time zones. Then, exhausted after a minimum time layover, she had to fly back. Even when she got home after a six-day trip, she felt like a zombie for the next two days. Long-haul international flying is not for the faint of heart.

Kerri took deep breaths, looked around the skipper's office for a clock, then let her shoulders relax.

"Drink this water. You look like hell." Stacey handed her a big water bottle.

"Thank you." Kerri chugged the liquid from heaven.

"Do you think you can answer some questions, Kerri? And please call me Stacey."

"Yes, I think so. Is everyone from my raft all right? My flight attendant, Janine Case?"

"They're all fine. Only a few minor injuries. We were very lucky today."

"We sure were, thanks to you. How in the world did you find us?"

"I can't tell you. Let's just say it was a combination of navigation skills and dumb luck. Were you using a signal mirror at fifteen-minute intervals?"

Kerri smiled. "That was my captain's assistant, Mel. She's a very bright young passenger that I showed how to signal with the mirror. I wasn't aware she was still able to signal you. We were all in pretty bad shape by then, drifting right into that storm, and would all be dead now if you hadn't found us when you did."

"I was just doing my job. Please give my compliments to Mel. We saw her first SOS flashes about two hours from your position. She kept signaling regularly, so you have her to thank. I'd like to meet her."

"Do you know anything about the rest of my passengers and crew? Have they been found?" Kerri was desperate for information.

"They were all in a group, very near your last reported position, and a cargo ship picked them up about four hours after you crashed. Frankly, I was surprised any of you walked away. I thought we'd be lucky to even find any bodies."

Kerri exhaled a big sigh of relief. "By the way, it wasn't a crash. It was a water landing. That's why we were able to get off the plane and into the rafts." That distinction was an important detail to Kerri. She did not crash her 767.

"Why were you so far away from the other survivors? Did you know where we were? Were you trying to find my ship? Tell me the truth, Kerri."

Stacey stared at her, clearly waiting for an answer. She wasn't the type of commander you withheld information from.

"We drifted away from the other rafts because a dumb-shit passenger accidentally threw our sea anchor overboard. I had no idea your ship was out there, and I certainly didn't try to locate your position. Do you think we were trying to spy on you?" Kerri was indignant.

"Look. Don't take offense. I just had to ask, for my higher-ups. I didn't think that was the case, but I had to know. Being so far away from the other survivors made you look suspicious. If you lost your sea anchor, that would explain how your raft drifted so far away. You were in an area of strong ocean currents. We knew your position from your emergency-locator transmitter, but then we lost the signal. The last transmission was from a position inside the typhoon. I really expected all of you to be dead and that this would be a recovery mission, not a rescue. I'm glad I was wrong."

"So am I. But how did you find us after we lost our ELT?"

"I plotted your last known position and your ELT pings, then adjusted for the ocean currents and the wind movement from the typhoon. Basically, it was a wild-ass guess. I had to persuade my boss I had a chance of finding you, because they'd called off the search."

"Really? They gave up?" Kerri was crushed.

"You have to remember, you went down in the middle of the ocean, with a bad storm nearby. They had a search grid of three hundred square miles, and they looked for you for two days without even finding a life vest. I'm not supposed to talk to you about the accident. I've briefed my crew, and they won't ask you any questions. I just needed to know if you were trying to find my ship on purpose, because of our mission."

"Absolutely not. I have no idea what your mission is. We were just along for the ride, and the raft drifted into that huge storm." What was their mission? Was it classified? Maybe that was why they took her gun.

"I've also been advised to tell you not to discuss the accident with anyone. The NTSB will be waiting to interview you as soon as we land in Honolulu."

A cold chill moved down Kerri's spine. She was going from the frying pan right into the fire. As if surviving a water landing, aircraft evacuation, ditching, two days in a raft in the middle of a storm wasn't bad enough. Now she would have to survive the inquisition from the National Transportation Safety Board.

As the pilot in command, she would be blamed for this accident. The pilots are always blamed first. Kerri had no doubt about this. At least she was alive to give her side of the story.

CHAPTER SIXTEEN

Janine heard a door squeak and awoke instantly, alert and afraid, her heart pounding. She searched for a weapon, ready to fight.

"Hey, Janine. It's me, Kerri."

"Kerri?"

"Yes. I wanted to check on you. Lieutenant Morris told me you weren't feeling well. How are you?"

Kerri stepped into a cone of light, illuminating her beautiful smile. Janine sat up and reached for her, opening her arms wide. Kerri sat on the edge of the metal bed, pulling Janine into a tight hug. They held each other for a long minute.

Kerri caressed her back, and the tears of relief came. This time she didn't try to hold them back. Kerri held her, and rocked her, and said nothing as Janine shuddered into Kerri's uniform jacket.

After she caught her breath, Kerri murmured into her ear, "We're all right. We're safe. I've got you." Kerri repeated her reassurances softly until Janine pulled her head up.

"I'm okay now. Thank you. Oh, look. I've made a mess of your jacket." Janine touched a big smear of makeup.

"What? My jacket's dirty? Well, you'll be getting a cleaning bill for that, miss."

"Oh, yeah? Just look at my uniform dress. It's in tatters. You owe me a new uniform."

"I guess we're even, then. I'm starving. Let's go find some food."

They lurched through the corridors of the ship, holding on to the handrails because of the rough seas, and found the noisy mess hall. It was a compact, utilitarian room packed with her passengers, all of them stuffing their faces. As Kerri and Janine got in line for the food, the noise level in the room lowered to dead quiet. Mr. Shapiro, who was discussing something with a group of passengers crowded around his table, glared at them and stopped talking. Janine was very conscious of being stared at, which was another uncomfortable feeling from her past. Panic started to rise in her throat.

"Kerri, let's come back later, when it's less crowded."

"No. We're both hungry, and we need to eat. They can just make room for us." Janine heard an edge of anger in Kerri's voice. The thought of Kerri unleashing a torrent of anger against their passengers made her shiver.

"Please, Kerri. I don't feel comfortable here. Let's go." Janine stopped, unmovable.

"All right. We'll leave and try again later."

Lieutenant Morris came up to them. "Oh, here you are. The skipper told me to find you and take you to her quarters. Please follow me."

He led them to a relatively quiet part of the ship, up a deck, then down a corridor ending at a door with "Lt. Cmdr. Stacey Gentry" on it.

"Oh, good. You're here. Come on in." Stacey opened her door for them. "It's not too big, but it's all we have left. There's a single bed over here, and the chair lays flat into another bed. There are sheets and towels on the desk. I left you both some clean dungarees, and this is the only stateroom with a private head. I'm also sending some food up for you, so enjoy, ladies."

Stacey pulled the door closed behind her and was gone in a flash.

Janine sat down in the chair, and Kerri maneuvered to the bed.

"I can't believe she gave us her room. This crew is amazing." Kerri looked around the tidy space.

"Do you mind if I shower first? This is the dirtiest I've ever been."

"Go right ahead. I'll just rest my eyes for a minute while you're in the shower." Kerri lay back on the bed and immediately started snoring.

Janine took the longest, hottest shower of her life. When she returned to the room, Kerri was dead asleep. She took a moment to stare at Kerri's smooth face, with only a few lines across her forehead. A couple of strands of gray at her temples stood out in her otherwise dark, silky hair. *Her face is beautiful when she's relaxed in sleep.*

She would let Kerri rest on the bed and, hopefully, sleep through the night. She carefully removed Kerri's shoes, then draped a blanket over her.

Janine wolfed down a ham-and-cheese sandwich, a chocolate-pudding cup, and another big bottle of water. She reclined the chair and made it up as a single bed.

"Well, it's more comfortable than the 767 crew bunk," she said to herself and looked over at Kerri. "Sleep well, my captain."

Janine pulled the blanket over her shoulder and muttered the silent prayer she said every night. *Please, God, keep Molly safe, and no dreams for me. Amen.*

❖

Kerri felt something next to her. "Move over."

"What?" Kerri's head was throbbing, and she was disoriented.

"Move over, Kerri. I'm freezing."

Kerri complied, rolled onto her side, and pressed herself

against the wall. Janine snuggled in next to her, pressing her backside into Kerri's lap. *Oh, my.*

Janine took Kerri's hand in hers and pulled Kerri's arm across her body.

Kerri didn't resist, because she really liked it, but she was confused. Everything Janine had told her about Molly, her ex-husband, and her refusal to return her calls didn't match up with Janine's actions now.

Maybe she really is cold and only wants to be close to stay warm. But it didn't feel that way to Kerri. Janine sought out Kerri to touch her, to physically connect with her. Kerri's desire for Janine was probably misplaced, as it had been before. Janine was very clear that she didn't care for a relationship, or even a date, with anyone. Kerri resisted the urge to pull her closer, even though she craved her. She wouldn't make any unwanted overtures. They both needed sleep, so Kerri kept her arm around Janine's waist, enjoying the feel of her body, and let herself fall back asleep. If anything happened between them, Janine would have to make the first move.

❖

Janine nestled against Kerri and tried to relax for the first time in a very long while. She'd lost the ability to sleep soundly when she was with Ryan. She'd trained herself to be a very light sleeper around him because he was either drunk, or high, most of the time, and because of his constant demand for bizarre, violent sex after they were married.

Now she was exhausted but couldn't sleep. Every time she drifted off, the trauma lurked just under the surface, waiting to get her. She knew what was happening with her mind but was helpless to stop it. Conjuring up the image of her kind therapist, Christine, she tried to recite the mantra she'd learned: "I am a free person. He can't hurt me anymore. I did not cause this. I am loved."

The words that had been a beam of light during her darkest moments seemed to fail her this time. She knew her fear from the raft ordeal was triggering her previous PTSD, but her usual coping mechanisms weren't enough. The only thing she could hang on to was Kerri.

Despite everything they'd been through, she still trusted Kerri with her life. Kerri would protect her, no matter what.

"Am I keeping you awake? I can move to the chair." Kerri's voice sounded husky with sleep.

"No. You're not keeping me awake, and I prefer you right here." She pulled Kerri's arm tighter around her.

"You're tossing and turning, and I thought I was disturbing you."

"I'm having trouble getting to sleep. It's just the old demons again. Sorry."

"There's nothing to be sorry about. We both just went through hell. I could call sick bay and see if they have any sleeping pills, if you want?"

"No, thanks. I can't take any of that stuff, and neither should you. The first thing they're going to do when we step off this boat is drug test us."

"You're right about that. Does anything help you? Hot chocolate? That always works for me."

"Sounds nice, but I'll just try my breathing exercises. If I'm bothering you, I'll go back to the chair."

"You're fine right here." Kerri snuggled closer. "How about a back rub? That might help you relax and go to sleep."

"A back rub? Really? That has to be the oldest line in the book." Janine couldn't help but laugh. "Is that how you got the nickname 'Don Juanita,' with lines like that?"

"I'm only talking about a therapeutic back rub. No strings attached. I promise."

"Sure. Why not? I'm too tired to fight." Janine pulled her shirttail out of her dungaree pants and rolled over so she lay facedown.

"Sorry. I don't have any oil."

Kerri slipped off her jacket, turned onto her side, and slid her hand slowly under Janine's shirt. After making small, light circles at Janine's waist with just her fingertips, she moved up her spine. Janine exhaled and tried to focus only on the lines Kerri was drawing on her skin. Her touch was soft and gentle, and a vision of skiers making snow trails on a virgin slope came to mind. The tightness in her shoulders started to release.

"Your neck and shoulder muscles are as hard as rocks. Would you like me to try to loosen those spasms? I'll have to press harder, so is that okay?" Kerri's voice was as soothing as her hands.

"Yes. Please do."

As Kerri's strong hands squeezed and massaged her tight muscles, Janine couldn't stop the small moans emerging from deep within her throat. Kerri's hands were magical as she kneaded the sore spots. Tingles ran down her spine from the firm yet soft strokes across her back. The anxiety from earlier disappeared, as did her fear of the dark.

Janine continued to lie on the bed soaking up tenderness coming through Kerri's fingers. She would lie there and let Kerri touch her as long as she could. She thought of their first back rub, when Janine was sunburned after their snorkeling trip. Kerri had been so gentle and kind on that occasion, and that experience had led to their first kiss on the flight deck. *That was so yummy.*

She melted into Kerri's caresses across her back. Her lips tingled with the memory of Kerri's velvet-soft lips opening for her. She wanted more kisses like that, a lot more. The heat of desire rose up from somewhere deep within her, and she didn't fight it this time. She let her hips gyrate against Kerri's lap.

"Um, Janine, are you trying to tell me something? Or am I misreading things?"

"You're not misreading anything. It feels so good to have you touch me."

The desire in Janine's belly was now a consuming fire she

could no longer ignore. She slowly rolled toward Kerri, gazed into her eyes, then reached for Kerri's face with her hands and pulled her down to kiss her. Kerri's lips were just as soft and luscious as she remembered. Janine opened her mouth for more. The tip of Kerri's tongue danced across her lower lip, then slowly entered her hungry mouth. Their kisses grew more fervent.

One of Kerri's hands was still beneath Janine's shirt, and she moved it up along the side of Janine's ribs. She realized what Kerri's target was and was eager to feel Kerri's hand on her breast. She wrapped her arms around Kerri's shoulders and pulled her on top. The weight of Kerri's body pressing against her own made Janine swoon. They fit together like puzzle pieces. Kerri continued to kiss her with more intensity as she moved her hand over Janine's breast.

"Oh, my God, that feels amazing," Janine murmured.

Kerri pressed her thigh between Janine's legs, and Janine kissed her harder.

Kerri surprised her when she broke their kiss. "Are you sure you want this?"

"I'm not sure of anything right now. I just want to keep kissing you."

Kerri answered her with more passionate kisses, and then she started to unbutton and remove Janine's blue dungaree shirt. Janine was a little scared, but excited, and Kerri's strong hands squeezing her breasts as she kissed her made Janine feel like she was floating on air. It had been so long since anyone had caressed her breasts with tenderness. She was hungry for more, and she wanted to taste Kerri's flesh.

"Take your shirt off."

Kerri quickly removed her uniform shirt and bra, revealing perfect, medium-sized breasts with hardened peaks. Janine lowered her head to taste the tempting nipples. She sucked a dark-mauve tip into her mouth and swirled her tongue all around it. The sound of Kerri's moans made Janine throb inside. She caressed Kerri's breasts as she feasted on them.

Kerri emitted a deep sound and pressed her breasts farther into Janine's mouth. Janine devoured her and wanted so much more.

A sharp rap at the door interrupted their passion. "Captain Sullivan?"

"Yes?" Kerri answered curtly.

"It's Lieutenant Morris. The skipper needs to see you in her office. I'm supposed to escort you. I'll wait outside the door until you're ready."

"Thank you, Lieutenant. I'll be right there." Kerri grumbled her reply, clearly unhappy at having to leave. "I'm so sorry. I'll come back as soon as I can."

Kerri threw on her clothes, then came over to Janine. "I'd like to continue where we left off, if that's okay." She gave Janine a dazzling smile.

"Of course. Me too."

They shared a sweet kiss one more time, and then Kerri left.

After Janine heard the door latch, the scent of Kerri's skin lingered, and she pulled a pillow next to her breasts, wishing it were Kerri.

❖

Friday, May 9

Kerri was very uncomfortable as she quickly marched to the skipper's office. Her arousal made her very sensitive, and her uniform slacks were rubbing. "Ow."

"Are you all right, ma'am?"

"Yes. I'm fine. Just tired."

Damn it...I bet my neck and face are bright red too. Stacey Gentry will know exactly what we've been up to. Oh, well, she's probably jealous.

"Here you go, ma'am. Have a nice day." Lieutenant Morris did an about-face and was off.

Stacey opened her door before Kerri even knocked.

"Kerri, come in, please. Why don't you sit on the couch with me? Would you like a drink?"

"I didn't think alcohol was allowed on navy ships. And, yes, I'd love one."

Stacey pulled out a bottle of Jameson whiskey from her lower desk drawer, then joined her on the couch.

"I need to tell you something, and I wish I didn't have to. But you're on my ship now, and you're my responsibility."

Kerri's insides tightened, like she was ready for a blow.

"Go ahead, Skipper."

"I've heard scuttlebutt on the ship about your passengers."

"What do you mean?"

"A David Shapiro, from Los Angeles, has been approaching all the other passengers about starting a class-action lawsuit against your airline, and against you personally."

That news didn't surprise Kerri. He'd been a thorn in her side since they first ditched the airplane.

"Thanks for telling me. I'll talk to him later and straighten everything out. I had to pull my gun on him in the raft, and he's pissed at me about it. I'll apologize and promise him substantial compensation from my company."

"It's not just that. He got a satellite phone from one of the researchers and called the press."

"Well, I was kind of expecting that too. Not too many people survive a water landing, so I'm sure the news media will be interested. Thank you for filling me in. I appreciate the heads-up."

"Anytime, Kerri. I checked your service record and saw you had a very distinguished air force career, as did your father. I just didn't want you walking into a buzz saw."

"Thanks, Stacey."

"Oh, by the way, my yeoman will pick up your uniform, and Janine's, and clean them up. They look pretty bad. He can't work magic, but he can improve their appearance."

Kerri let out a big sigh of relief. Being called into the commander's office was never pleasant, but she was happy she'd made a new friend in Stacey.

She entered the skipper's cabin as quietly as she could.

"Kerri? Is that you?"

"Yes. It's me."

"Come over here." Janine opened her arms and made room on the bed, then flipped on the light. "What did the skipper want?"

"She told me Mr. Shapiro is trying to organize the passengers into suing me and that he'd alerted the press about it."

"That piece of crap. And I was so nice to him."

"Well, at least we're around to tell the truth. I'm not surprised. We did an amazing job of dealing with multiple emergencies—ditching the plane and keeping our passengers alive in a raft for days. I think we'll be fine."

Kerri's stomach growled.

"You never got any food, did you?"

"I guess not. I think I'll clean up and change clothes. Then maybe we can go get something to eat."

The gentle touching from before was gone, like a clearing fog. Kerri had to push her romantic hopes for a morning alone with Janine to the back of her mind. There would be an investigation, a thorough and comprehensive examination of every aspect of her flying career, and of her entire life. *Oh, crap.*

CHAPTER SEVENTEEN

After stuffing themselves with a hot breakfast, Janine and Kerri went to the skipper's cabin again and slept for another seven hours. A familiar knock at the door awakened them.

"Yes, Lieutenant Morris. What is it?"

"Captain Sullivan and Miss Case, I have your uniforms. I'll just hang them outside the door. Also, the skipper said to inform you that we will be arriving in Honolulu in four hours."

"Thank you, Lieutenant."

Janine felt Kerri get up, and a cold wind chilled her back.

"Where are you going?"

"To the lav, except the navy calls it a head."

Janine was still exhausted, even after her big meal and hours of sleep.

"I'm going back to sleep. Wake me when we hit the top of descent point."

Kerri came over to the side of the bed and bent down close to Janine's ear. "I have a better idea. Let's go up to the bridge and watch for Oahu. It's a beautiful island."

They combed their hair, tucked in their dungaree shirts, then walked to the stairs that led to the bridge. The door was open, with a brisk ocean breeze flowing through the panoramic windows. Stacey, who was sitting in her skipper's chair, turned to them and gestured them in.

The view from the bridge windows was spectacular. The ocean was deep blue with small, occasional whitecaps. The sky was Janine's favorite color, the pale blue of Molly's eyes. Sunlight danced on the water like glittering diamonds. The ocean looked so peaceful and beautiful from here, so different from the menacing water they'd had to deal with on their raft. Janine shuddered at her memory.

"Is it all right if we just sit here for a while?" Kerri asked Stacey.

"Sure. Help yourself to some coffee."

Watching the horizon gently move up and down from the bridge of this ship helped Janine relax and center herself. In her job as a flight attendant, she'd trained herself to talk to strangers, smile, and be friendly to everyone. She genuinely liked most people, but she was always on alert.

Janine felt safe in an airplane, maybe because it was an enclosed space, or maybe because she knew no one could harm her while she was flying in the sky. Many people were afraid to fly, and she certainly understood fear, but she could use her calming manner and kind touch to help people overcome their anxiety.

They hadn't seen many of their passengers, because they'd been sleeping so much. Janine could barely contain her excitement at the thought of seeing Molly. The company would have contacted Rosa, her emergency person, and flown them from LA to Honolulu. She couldn't let herself think about Molly, or she'd start to cry.

But she could think about one thing, and that was Kerri's luscious mouth. A shiver ran through her belly at the remembrance of Kerri's tongue in her mouth and Kerri's hands on her breasts.

For the first time in three years, Janine allowed herself to think about the possibility of a real relationship. Maybe Kerri Sullivan was the woman she was supposed to meet to change the direction of her life. She liked her quiet, small life with Molly, but she did long for someone to love. And she wanted a woman. Her brief foray into heterosexual marriage had been disastrous, with the exception of Molly.

Last night with Kerri confirmed that she had real feelings only for women. She loved the feel of Kerri's strong body, her amazing hands, and her delicious lips. As soon as they docked in Honolulu and got through the madhouse of the press, she couldn't wait to go to the crew hotel, take Kerri to her room, and finish what they'd started in the skipper's cabin.

Kerri pointed straight ahead. "There's Oahu."

It was only a dark speck on the horizon, but it meant seeing Molly. As the ship grew closer, Janine could make out more details of the island.

"I can see Diamond Head." Kerri squeezed her arm. She was as excited as a new tourist, and she flashed that dazzling smile again. Janine's stomach did flip-flops when she sat next to Kerri and felt the heat of her body. Only now did Janine allow herself to believe this was real, that they would truly be able to go home and be safe.

"Thanks for visiting, but we have to get busy now. Please return to your cabin and get ready for arrival," Stacey said.

Janine and Kerri hurried back to the skipper's cabin and changed into their clean uniforms. Stacey's yeoman had done an amazing job of cleaning them.

Kerri took Janine's hands in her own. "I have to talk to you before we get off this boat and face a throng of people. Let's sit down."

Kerri's hands were so warm she wanted to hold onto them forever.

"I realize we've been through a life-threatening event, but I know what I feel. I want to be with you, Janine. You've had a very difficult past, but that doesn't matter to me. I care about you, and I want to see if we have a future together. I really hope you feel the same way."

Janine looked into Kerri's eyes, and love surrounded her heart. It was the first time she'd ever had that sensation.

"Yes, Kerri. I feel the same way about you. I trust you, and I'm willing to try."

As Janine spoke those words for the first time ever, a weight lifted off her shoulders.

"Attention, all crew," the PA blared. "Report to stations for docking. Passengers, please stay in the staterooms until we tell you we are ready to disembark."

"I guess we're getting close. I want to introduce you to my daughter, Molly."

"Are you sure you want her to meet me now? It's okay if you want to spend tonight with her. I'll certainly understand."

"You're right. That might be a lot for one day. But I want her to meet you soon. You're very important to me."

She moved closer, wrapped her arms around Kerri's neck, and kissed her slowly, longingly, passionately. She wanted every second with her before they had to face the world.

❖

"All passengers, report to the port side, main deck, to disembark."

"Ready?" Janine asked.

Kerri didn't want this moment to end. She could get lost in her kisses and spend the rest of her days caressing Janine's soft skin. She admired Janine's other physical assets, but her attraction consisted of so much more than just desire for a beautiful woman. Kerri had learned an amazing amount about her, in such a short period of time, that she felt like they'd been together for a long time. They'd learned to read each other's moods, they both had tender hearts, and they both had never found real love.

Kerri had seen the true Janine when they'd stood together at the abyss of death. She wasn't afraid of the prospect of her own demise, thinking only of her beloved daughter. When they had nothing left on the raft and only their strength of character remained, Janine had shown great courage and compassion. Kerri was so proud of her.

Now it was the time to face the music, but she wasn't looking forward to it. During her flying career, she'd never sought the spotlight. She wasn't interested in publicity or fame. She'd always valued being an excellent pilot, doing a good job, and flying a safe aircraft. She was a dedicated leader who always took care of her crew. Now, she felt uncertain of what to expect when she walked off this ship.

Both Kerri and Janine would be questioned, but she was proud of the way they'd kept their passengers alive and signaled for their rescue. She was also looking forward to meeting Mel's parents and telling them what a great girl she was.

Everyone would face a big challenge during the next few weeks while the accident was investigated. At least she would be going through this ordeal with Janine. They'd survived at sea, and she was confident they could survive anything.

"Let's go."

They left the small stateroom together. She would miss this safe place Stacey Gentry had given them.

A mass of humanity waited for them at the end of the gangway, with camera lights flashing, boom microphones thrust in Kerri's face, and reporters shouting questions. The tumult overwhelmed her.

A large man came up to her. "I'm from the FAA. Please come with me." He held her upper arm, indicating that she was going nowhere.

Kerri looked back at Janine and saw her look of surprise. She followed Janine's line of sight to a beautiful redheaded little girl being held up in the air so she could see over the crowd. *That must be Molly. But who's he?*

She looked back at Janine and saw fear on her face.

Oh, my God. That must be Ryan.

Kerri's fingers clenched into fight fists. She wanted to go over there and beat his smug face in. Company managers surrounded Janine, then led her away.

This was not the hero's welcome Kerri had hoped for.

A black SUV was waiting for them, and the FAA guy opened the back door for her. Kerri was thrilled to see her old friend, Camille Hughes, sitting in the back seat, and they hugged for a long time.

"We were so worried about you, Kerri." Camille kissed Kerri's cheek.

"I'm really glad to see you. What's going on? Am I supposed to make a statement?"

"Everything's fine. This is just the normal process for any aircraft mishap. That's why I'm here. They pulled me off a four-day Hong Kong trip to meet you first, and to help guide you through this maze. I'm a volunteer with our union's Critical Incident Response Program."

Kerri let out a big breath.

"Here's what's going to happen next. We're taking you to a private lab for toxicology and drug testing. Do you need more water to drink? Then you see the doc, and after that, we go to your hotel room, where I have fresh uniforms for you and a great hair and makeup lady."

"No, I don't need any water, and why do I need help with my hair and makeup?"

"You're going to have to stand in front of the press and make a public statement. Don't you want to look your best? And don't forget, you're representing all us pilots at Trans Global."

They pulled up to the rear entrance of a nondescript, windowless building. The FAA man opened the car door, then said something to a woman in a white lab coat.

"Please come with me, Captain Sullivan," the woman asked.

Kerri followed her, filled out forms, peed in a cup, blew into a breathalyzer, and was stabbed in the arm for a blood sample. This was the protocol for any aircraft accident, but it still humiliated and irritated her. There was no presumption of innocence here. All pilots had to prove they were not guilty.

"Next stop, the doc." Camille opened a door to another hall.

"I don't need to see a doctor." Kerri was starting to get pissed off.

Camille stopped, turned to Kerri, and stood very close to her face. "You need to stow that attitude right now. I understand that you've been through hell, but everyone is going to interrogate you before you get through this. That means the FAA, the NTSB, Boeing, our union safety committee, doctors, and our own company management. You need to be one hundred percent cooperative."

"I know, Camille. I'm just really tired. I need a drink and a quiet hotel room."

"Kerri, you clearly have no idea what you're walking into."

Camille pushed Kerri into a ladies' restroom, then locked the door. "You've been in the news for three days. Every detail of your life is all over the internet. Everyone in the world has seen every picture you ever posted on Facebook, your complete military record, your flying history, even a video of you talking to a kindergarten class about flying—which was great, by the way."

"Oh, my God. I expected some press, but not this."

"Kerri, whether you like it or not, you're a celebrity. You will have zero privacy for the next several months. Everywhere you go, every word you say will be recorded. Therefore, you will not be going to a bar for a drink, now or any time, because someone will take a picture of you drinking. You need to be very cognizant of this fact and of whom you represent."

"Shit. I don't need this right now." Kerri was shaking.

Camille wrapped her arms around her. "Come here, honey."

After a few moments, Kerri composed herself, washed her face, smoothed out her uniform jacket, and stood tall.

"All right. Let's get this visit to the doctor over with."

Kerri walked out of the ladies' restroom with her head held high. After what she'd survived, she could get through anything.

After the doctor's exam, they drove Kerri to the crew hotel. Instead of a regular room, they had her in a suite with the hair and makeup lady, who was waiting for her. It felt good to take a long, hot shower and put on a new uniform. Kerri gazed at herself in the mirror, surprised by what she saw. Dark circles under her eyes made her pale skin color appear unhealthy.

"I look like death warmed over," she told the woman who was scrutinizing her.

"Don't worry about that. I'll get you just like your old self again. I'm Kalani, and I'm here to make you gorgeous."

"Thank you, Kalani. I don't need to look gorgeous, but I would like to appear normal again."

Kerri closed her eyes as Kalani ran her fingers along her scalp and started styling her hair. She tried to relax, but the image of fear on Janine's face kept returning. Why was Ryan here with Janine's daughter? What did he intend to do?

Based on Janine's response when she first spotted him, he was an unwelcome surprise. Kerri's own reaction to him had startled her. Her instinct to smash in his face with her fists was still very strong. After listening to Janine describe her relationship with him, Kerri wanted to hurt him as badly as he hurt Janine. Men who beat women were worthless human beings who deserved to be in prison.

"How's that?" Kalani asked.

Kerri examined her image in the mirror. "Wow. You're really talented. I haven't looked this good in years. Thank you, Kalani."

A knock sounded at the door, and Camille went to answer it. The chief pilot of the entire company, Captain Ross Wheeler, walked into her room. Kerri knew who he was, but she'd never met him. He shook hands with Camille, then came over to her.

"How are you, Kerri? I'm so happy you and your crew and passengers are safe."

His concern felt genuine, and he reached out to shake her hand. Kerri gave his big hand a firm grip.

"I'm glad to be here, Ross. Actually, I'm glad to be anywhere, and thanks for asking."

"We've prepared a draft of a statement for you to read to the press. You can look it over, but I need you to stick to it."

Kerri read the paper he handed her. It was a standard "thank you for your support" statement and concluded with a line that she would not be able to take any questions, due to the ongoing investigation. "This looks good to me, Ross."

"So tell me what happened, Kerri?"

Ross sounded sincere, but Kerri was wary about speaking to him. She knew every word she said would be scrutinized and that his priority was to protect the company. She had to be careful not to say anything incriminating.

"We'd just passed the midpoint on our route over the ocean, when I heard and felt a big boom. Then we lost all cabin pressure. While dealing with that emergency, I realized we'd also lost the right engine and that the shrapnel from the engine must have punctured both wing fuel tanks. We were losing fuel, and we didn't have enough gas to make it to Hilo, so we had to ditch the jet in the water and evacuate."

"Incredible. Well, we'll have the opportunity to go into detail later. For now, just read your statement to the press, and then you'll meet with the FAA and NTSB folks for a few more questions."

Kerri suspected he knew she was being intentionally vague.

"One more thing. Make sure you're completely truthful with them. Don't leave anything out, and don't try to hide anything. That would be very bad for you."

This would be the only friendly warning she would get.

"I understand, Ross. Thanks for stopping by to see me. How's the rest of my crew, and my passengers?"

"They're all fine. You did a good job. Call me if I can help in any way."

Kerri took his business card. "Thanks."

"Kerri, we need to leave for the press conference. Are you ready?" Camille asked.

"Yes. I think I am."

Kerri wanted to put this behind her, and she wanted to see Janine. She was worried about her. By the look on her face, Janine was surprised and unhappy to see Ryan, especially holding her daughter. Why was her husband here if they were separated? His intentions toward Janine were most likely not good. She'd only glanced at him, and he wasn't a big guy. Instead, he was very average-looking except for his obviously expensive suit. She still had a powerful desire to smash his face in for what he'd done to Janine.

But she couldn't allow herself to worry about Janine. She had to appear before the press and make a good impression on behalf of her company and all women airline pilots everywhere. Whenever there was an aircraft accident with a woman pilot flying, people judged all female pilots by her performance, good or bad.

Camille led her to the hotel convention center through the kitchen entrance, so the press wouldn't see her.

Kerri peeked through a door at the room, which was packed with reporters and television crews. *I really don't care for this.*

Camille touched her elbow. "It's time. Let's go, and remember to just read the statement."

They walked out to a dais with a bank of microphones in front of her, and Kerri sat in the middle of a table facing the crowd. She felt like she was part of the Spanish Inquisition. She waited as her boss addressed the crowd.

"Good afternoon, ladies and gentlemen. I'm Captain Ross Wheeler, chief pilot of Trans Global Airlines, and we'd like to welcome you to this press conference. We are so relieved that all the passengers and crew of Trans Global flight 401 are safe and unhurt after their in-flight emergency. Trans Global, the FAA, and the NTSB will carry out a complete investigation. I would like to introduce Captain Kerri Sullivan, the pilot in command of flight 401, who did an excellent job of landing her crippled 767 aircraft on the ocean and successfully completed an evacuation and ditching. Please welcome Captain Sullivan."

Kerri heard muted applause in the huge room.

After she read her prepared statement, many reporters raised their hands to ask questions.

Ross took the microphone and repeated that no questions would be taken. Then he turned to Kerri. "Let's go."

As they were leaving the dais, a reporter shouted, "Captain Sullivan, did you intentionally shut down an engine so you could land on the water and ditch the plane? Why did you do it?"

Kerri stopped immediately. Though she wasn't supposed to answer any questions, she couldn't let this egregious remark pass.

She grabbed the microphone. "That's an insane thing to say. Under no circumstances would I shut down an engine on purpose. It blew up, we had multiple emergencies, and we're lucky to be alive. Get your facts straight."

"Come on, Kerri. We need to go now." Ross took her elbow to lead her off the dais.

As he rushed her out of the room, Kerri heard another reporter yell. "Hey, Captain. The facts are that the engine was operating normally before you shut it down. How do you explain that?"

"What the hell?" Kerri started to turn back to the microphone.

Ross stopped her. "Leave it. We'll discuss this in the hotel room."

She knew better than to defy him again. She wouldn't win this battle.

By the time they got back to her room, Kerri was furious. "Ross, what the hell did that reporter mean when he said the engine was operating normally? How could he possibly know anything about my engines? I need you to tell me right now what's going on here."

"Calm down, Kerri. We're not supposed to discuss anything before the NTSB debriefs you."

Kerri stood before her boss with her hands on her hips, waiting for him to answer her. She took a deep breath. "Do not tell me to calm down. What the fuck did that reporter mean?"

"All right. Here's what happened. Flight 401 has been in the news nonstop for the last several days. Someone was able to hack into our aircraft maintenance computer system. They found the tail number of the aircraft and the engine telemetry data from both engines that the jet transmitted automatically right before your emergency. It showed that both engines were operating within normal parameters. The hacker released the engine data to the public."

"Of course they were. I'd just checked all the engine gauges when we passed the midpoint. They were both fine, but then all hell broke loose. Didn't the company explain that?"

"Kerri, we can't officially say anything until the investigation is complete."

"Well, that's bullshit."

"Sorry, but that's the process. Kerri, you cannot respond when reporters shout questions at you or say outrageous, insulting things to you. You have to stay above the fray. Hold your head up, try to look professional and dignified, because you're still representing us."

"I got it. Mind my *P*s and *Q*s and keep my mouth shut." She sat down in a huff.

Camille walked over and turned on the television. "Let's see what they're saying about us today."

The commentator announced, "Breaking news. Captain Kerri Sullivan, of the mysterious Trans Global 401 flight, denies she did anything wrong with the engines, up until the moment the plane crashed and sank in the ocean. This happened at the news briefing today by her company, Trans Global Airlines."

"He completely misrepresented what I said."

"Oh, just wait until all the talking heads jump in with their own bizarre conspiracy theories." Camille's words didn't make Kerri feel any better.

The commentator spoke again. "In happier news from flight 401, here is the last crew member rescued, Flight Attendant Janine Case, reunited with her family. Let's hear from her husband, Ryan Jackson."

Kerri kept her eyes glued to the screen to look at this guy and to hear what he'd say about Janine.

He stood before the camera with a single tear at the corner of his eye.

The reporter asked, "How do you feel, Mr. Jackson?"

He paused, looked down, then tearfully replied, "My daughter, Molly, and I are so happy to have Jan back with us. It's a miracle, and we're so thankful to God. We just want to go home to Chicago, let Jan recuperate from her injuries, and be a family again. Thank you all for your prayers."

Kerri was transfixed as she stared at Janine. Her face looked like a plastic mask, with a small, frozen smile and darting eyes. Who was she searching for? Was she looking for an escape route? Worst of all was seeing his arm around her shoulders, his fingers digging into the tender flesh of her shoulder.

Kerri wanted to scream and kill him.

CHAPTER EIGHTEEN

Janine was trying her best not to panic. The cameras, boom mikes, noise, and crowds made her very anxious.

"Mommy, you're hurting my hand."

"I'm sorry, Pumpkin. How about if I pick you up, so you can see better."

"Okay, Mommy."

Molly reached up to her, and she bent down, picked up her little girl, and positioned Molly between herself and Ryan. She held on to Molly as if her life depended on it. In desperation, she forced herself to do a four-count breath exercise so she wouldn't hyperventilate.

Just a few more seconds. It'll be over soon. Hang in there. You can get through this.

If she focused on her mantras and continued to breathe, she knew she'd be all right. She was familiar with the routine of dealing with Ryan. He'd been very clear when he'd warned her to not say anything if asked. And she knew very well the consequences of defying him, which weren't pretty.

Janine pasted on her well-practiced, modest smile as she stood before the press. Ryan's strong grip on the top of her shoulder meant he expected her to stand politely and not say a word. She couldn't help but look for Kerri. She scanned the crowd repeatedly, desperate to find the face she trusted, the face she needed—Kerri's face.

Janine had asked about her, and the flight attendant managers explained that she was in a different location until the NTSB completed its debriefings. Hers was scheduled for tomorrow morning and would last all day. Maybe she'd get lucky and run into Kerri in the debriefing room.

Ryan squeezed her shoulder hard and said, "Let's get out of here."

Janine looked around the crowd one more time, hoping to see Kerri. She wasn't here. Where was she? Why hadn't she called? Ryan had confiscated the phone they'd issued to her and monitored all her calls. He hadn't done anything insane or violent yet, but she knew his viciousness was still there, just under the surface.

They returned to her hotel room, where Ryan bolted and chained the door closed.

"Thank you, Mommy and Molly. You guys were both great today." He wore that sick smile.

"Molly, why don't you go into the bedroom and lie down for your nap. Mommy and Daddy need to talk."

"I don't need a nap. I'm not tired."

"Molly, don't make me angry. Go lie down now." His voice was threatening.

He reached for the buckle of his wide leather belt, so Janine ran over to Molly, scooped her up, turned her back to block him, and hurried her into the bedroom. She had to make Molly comply.

"Pumpkin, you have to lie here, be quiet, and try to go to sleep, or Daddy will get very mad."

"I don't care. I don't like him. Why can't we go home?"

"We'll get home soon, but for now, you have to do what he says, or he'll hurt us. Do you understand? It's very important that you do." Janine pulled her into a hug and cried into her small neck. "I'm so sorry about all of this. I wish it was different, but for now, we have to pretend to go along with Daddy. Will you do that for me?"

"Yes, Mommy, I will. But I still don't like him."

"Me either."

Janine went back into the sitting room to talk to Ryan. "She's lying down. All this has confused her."

"Her manners haven't improved since I let her live with you. She needs some hard discipline to make her shut that smart mouth."

Janine cringed at his ugly tone of voice.

"Jan, darling, we have more important things to talk about." He flashed her a smile with his perfect veneers. "I was devastated when I thought I'd lost you. Then when they found you, I felt like we've been given a second chance. I want us to try to be a family again."

Hearing these words from him stunned her. After all the terrible things he'd said and done to her in the past, now he expected her to believe him? She knew better than to interrupt him with a question. She kept her face expressionless and listened.

"There's one more thing. I've decided to run for Congress. I need you and Molly to move back to Chicago and live with me. Nothing will change about our current arrangement. I have an image to maintain and need everyone to see that I'm a good family man. You understand, of course."

She certainly did. With his newfound political ambition, he planned to make her, and Molly, his prisoners again.

Janine would die before she'd let that happen.

❖

Saturday, May 10

After a fitful night, Kerri woke up exhausted. She couldn't get that image of Janine, with Ryan's grip on her shoulder, out of her mind. What was he doing to her and Molly? Worry for both of them consumed her.

She was glad she'd been able to see Molly. Janine's daughter was a darling little girl, who clung to her mother's neck like a baby monkey. On the news show, Kerri noticed that Janine held on tight to Molly, and that she'd positioned Molly between herself and Ryan. Molly must be so confused by all this, especially when her estranged father had showed up.

Kerri had to see Janine. She remembered her cell phone number from when she'd stalked her and dialed it.

A strange man answered. "Who is this?" *Crap. That must be Ryan.*

Kerri hung up on him. She didn't intend to ever speak to him. She didn't like anything about him, and she wanted to get Janine and Molly away from him as fast as possible. Her ringing phone interrupted her rising fury.

"Good morning. I hope you're dressed and ready to go. Meet me in the lobby for coffee in ten minutes."

"Okay, Camille. I'll be down in a few."

Kerri hastily showered and dressed in her new Trans Global uniform. She made sure her lady's tie was even, and she straightened the insignia on her captain's hat. Camille had her sizes correct, but the slacks were loose on her hips. She hadn't even stepped on a scale to see how much weight she'd lost during their ordeal.

A vision of Janine, wearing her blue uniform dress and her black high heels, came into Kerri's mind. She was so beautiful that Kerri's breath caught. Kerri missed her. She missed sitting next to her on the raft. She missed lacing her fingers between Janine's. She missed the sound of her calm voice. Kerri missed kissing Janine. She really, really missed kissing her. Her lips were so full and luscious that Kerri could kiss them for days. Most of all, she missed looking into Janine's pale-blue eyes.

Kerri saw so much when she looked at Janine. She didn't just admire her beauty and her gorgeous body, but she saw the caution in Janine's eyes turn into trust. Kerri had witnessed a fierce determination to survive when they worked together on the raft. She's seen resigned sadness, but also grace, when they faced death together. Janine's inner strength gave Kerri the courage to not give up. Together, they claimed the will to live.

A sharp knock at the door interrupted Kerri's memory.

"Come on, Kerri. We have to go. I have coffee for you."

As she sipped it, she focused on what she would say at this debriefing. She also listened to Camille's advice in the car ride over to the NTSB field office, located in the Honolulu Federal Building.

"Only answer the direct question they're asking. Don't volunteer anything additional, unless they ask for it. Do not speculate on what might have caused the accident. That's their job. Keep your temper in check no matter what they say. This will all be filmed. Got it?"

"Yes, Camille. Thank you."

Kerri was very glad she'd gone through prisoner-of-war training in Air Force Survival School. This would be a hostile interrogation. Every word she uttered would be scrutinized.

After federal officers checked their credentials, Camille led her down a long corridor. She rounded the corner, saw Janine, and stopped completely. After they locked eyes for a long moment, they walked toward each other with outstretched arms. Kerri wrapped herself firmly against her and buried her face in Janine's neck.

"I've missed you so much." She inhaled Janine's perfume deeply.

"Oh, Kerri. I miss you too." Janine kept her tight grip on her.

"Are you all right?" She stepped back to look at Janine.

Janine pulled her into another big hug. "We're okay, but I need to talk to you."

"Jan! Get over here. You have to go in now." Ryan's voice was a threatening whisper.

Janine looked at her, one last time, before she entered the debriefing room for the flight attendants.

Kerri's heart sank in disappointment.

"Come on, Kerri. You're not supposed to speak to the other crew members until you finish your debrief." Camille led her to the pilots' debriefing room.

Kerri walked into a large conference room with three separate tables. The largest one stood at the front, with microphones on it and seven chairs around it. Kerri walked over to the table on the side, which held two microphones. Cameras were placed directly across from her to record her every word. She saw her first officer, Ray, gave him a hug, and sat next to him.

"This preliminary hearing will now come to order."

A silver-haired man in an expensive suit and tie pounded the table with a gavel.

"Good morning. I'm Robert Ellsworth, vice-chairman of the NTSB Aviation Division. We'd like to thank the representatives from Boeing and Trans Global Airlines for being here today. And, of course, we welcome Captain Kerri Sullivan and First Officer Ray Elliott. This is a preliminary hearing only to gather facts. We will not be providing any analysis or causal factors. Let's begin by swearing everyone in."

Kerri observed Robert Ellsworth carefully. He had a great deal of power over her life, and her flying career, and she understood that he would be deciding her fate. She had to impress him.

"Captain Sullivan, let's start with you. We've already examined your flight-training records, your medical files, and your accident history with the FAA and find nothing out of order with your qualifications or training. We've also reviewed the complete maintenance history of the aircraft, and everything was up to standards. Please tell us, in your own words, what happened on flight 401."

The entire room was silent, everyone waiting for her to speak. She took a sip of water, then told the full story of what occurred in the air and what led to the decision to ditch the aircraft. Kerri had begun to describe the aircraft evacuation and their time at sea in the raft, when Mr. Ellsworth interrupted her.

"Captain Sullivan. Let's return to your first indication that something was wrong. Tell us exactly what you saw, and in what order." Ellsworth was leaning forward in his seat, like he couldn't wait to hear what she had to say.

"As I already said, the first officer, Ray, was out of the flight deck using the restroom, and Flight Attendant Janine Case was the safety person on the flight deck with me. Ray gave us the signal that he was ready to come back to his seat, I put on my oxygen mask as required, Janine opened the cockpit door to let Ray in, and then all hell broke loose."

"It's important that you be more specific with your answers, Captain Sullivan. How, exactly, did all hell break loose?"

This guy intended to be relentless in his interrogation. She had to be very clear in stating her facts.

"First, I heard, and felt, a large boom, followed immediately by instant fog in the cockpit, and then the cabin-altitude warning horn sounded. The red master warning lights came on, and I realized we had an emergency decompression. While we were completing the emergency checklist, a few seconds later, I felt the aircraft slow and start rolling to the right. I looked at the engine gauges and confirmed we'd also lost the right engine."

Kerri was growing frustrated at having to repeat herself, so she took a drink of water and waited for the next question. She had to make an effort to keep her facial expression neutral. She could show no weakness before them, or they would shred her to pieces. Kerri tried hard to remember every word she'd said to them, so she wouldn't contradict herself.

Ellsworth turned to Ray. "First Officer Elliott, is that how you remember the sequence of events?"

"Ah, yes, sir, I believe so," Ray answered tenuously.

Kerri was shocked. He should have backed her up with more certainty.

"First Officer Elliott, do you *believe* Captain Sullivan's description of events is correct, or do you *know* they're correct?"

Ray was squirming in his seat and hesitated to answer.

"Do you want me to repeat the question?" Ellsworth sounded condescending.

"No, sir." Ray stammered. "It's just that I was a little fuzzy for a few seconds at the beginning of the emergency. But I'm sure Captain Sullivan's recall of the events is accurate."

"How can you be so positive, when you admit that your mind was fuzzy?"

"I don't know, sir." Ray hung his head.

"Let's get back to Captain Sullivan. Are you aware that the automatic-engine-reporting system transmitted data on the condition of both your engines just three minutes before the mishap occurred? Are you also aware that all the engine data was in the normal operating range?"

"Yes, sir. I'd just looked at both engine gauges when we crossed the halfway checkpoint on the route of flight, and they were fine."

"What happened to the right engine in the three minutes between a satisfactory engine report and a catastrophic disintegration that punctured the hull of your aircraft?"

"Mr. Ellsworth, I have no idea." Kerri had to count to three before she answered, so she wouldn't yell at him.

"Could a severe compressor stall cause an engine to disintegrate?"

Kerri hesitated. She didn't trust this old fucker as far as she could throw him. He was trying to trap her, but she had to answer truthfully.

"Yes, sir. That is possible."

"Good. I'm glad we agree on that point. Now, isn't it also possible that moving a throttle rapidly to idle power, then quickly back to max power, can cause an engine to compressor stall at thirty-five thousand feet?"

Kerri was fuming. Not only was Ellsworth questioning her skill as a pilot and her judgment as a captain, but he was trying to humiliate her by asking her elementary jet-engine questions in front of the cameras.

"Of course rapid throttle movement at cruise altitude can cause engine damage. That's why we have a warning in our flight manual. If you like, I can show you which page of the flight manual it's on."

"Thank you, but unnecessary. We already have that page from your company's flight manual. I just needed to confirm you were aware of that engine restriction."

Kerri was seething. She dug her nails into the palms of her hands to keep from screaming at him.

Camille spoke up. "Mr. Ellsworth, as a representative of the pilot's union, we object to you questioning Captain Sullivan about basic aircraft systems. If you have no further questions relevant to this investigation, I suggest you conclude this interview."

Kerri could hear grumbling in the seats behind her. Stealing a glance over her shoulder, she saw a packed room of reporters.

Ellsworth sat up in his seat, straightened his tie, adjusted his glasses, and tried to look dignified. "We will adjourn for today after one final question. Captain Sullivan, did you intentionally damage your right engine? Why would you do that?"

Kerri shot up from her seat. "No, sir. I absolutely did not damage my own engine. That's an idiotic suggestion, and no pilot would ever do that."

"We'll see, Captain Sullivan. We'll see. In the meantime, due to the possibility of pilot error in this mishap, you will surrender your Airline Transport Pilot license and your FAA Class One medical certificate. You are hereby suspended from any flying until the results of this investigation are known. You are also prohibited from leaving the country, and you will surrender your passport. I will find out the truth, no matter what it takes. You're dismissed."

Kerri felt like she'd been knifed in the chest. She'd worked her entire life to earn that license, and now it was being taken from her, possibly forever.

Chapter Nineteen

Janine made sure she was in the middle of a pack of flight attendants when they went to the restroom. She was desperate to see Kerri again and hoped she would run into her in the ladies' room. They were on a ten-minute break from their debriefings, and she had to get back soon. Only two of her crew members were left in the restroom, and she was sure Ryan would come looking for her any minute. *Come on, Kerri. Come to me.*

Just as the last two flight attendants were leaving, Kerri walked in, held up by another woman pilot, tears streaming down her cheeks.

"Oh, my God, Kerri. What happened?"

"They took my pilot's license."

Janine pulled Kerri into a full body hug and held her. "I'm so sorry. You didn't deserve that."

Camille jumped in. "I hate to break up this party, but a creepy guy's pacing outside the door."

"Please, Camille. Stall him as long as you can," Kerri pleaded.

"I'll try, but make it quick." Camille went out the door and blocked the entrance.

They held each other's face and kissed one another with a fierce hunger.

"Janine, I've been so worried about you. Are you and Molly all right? What does Ryan want?"

"Kerri, we're okay, but I have only a few seconds. I need you to hear me. I'm not afraid of him anymore. I will not let him control me or Molly. We may need to get out of the country very quickly, if I get a chance. I have an emergency phone number, for texting only. It's my phone number, plus the number eight-sixteen. When we're safe, I'll let you know where we are. I have to go."

Janine pulled Kerri's face to her own and kissed her again, then looked into Kerri's eyes. "I want a future with you, Kerri."

They heard the door opening. Janine shoved Kerri into a toilet stall and closed the door on her.

"Jan? You still in here? Everyone's leaving."

Janine turned on the faucet. "Be right there, Ryan."

She exited the restroom and walked away quickly with him so he wouldn't see Kerri.

Darkness lifted off her heart. She was actually happy inside. Seeing, touching, and kissing Kerri, even if just for a moment, made her feel connected again. She and Kerri had been to hell and back. If she had Kerri with her, she could survive anything, even Ryan, for a brief period.

Janine knew her time was very limited. Once Ryan got her back to his parents' mansion in Chicago, she and Molly would never be free of him. She needed outside help, and communication with Kerri would be very difficult. She could trust only one person who might be able to help her. Janine had to contact her mentor, and friend, Chief Purser George Cato. She would see George later tonight when her crew met at the hotel with the company egress training instructors. He respected Kerri as a captain. She only hoped he cared for her as a person too.

❖

Kerri waited until she could hear no more sound before she climbed down from the toilet seat and emerged from her bathroom stall. She relished having a moment to herself in the empty restroom. How had the second worst day of her life become the best day of it?

She was suspended indefinitely from flying, but now she knew Janine wanted a future with her. Considering that Janine had never returned any of her calls or texts, and they had almost died at sea, this was quite a turnaround. This was a huge change in Janine's attitude, and it gave her hope for a future with love instead of loneliness.

Camille was waiting for her as Kerri came out of the restroom. "We're going straight to the airport to fly you home."

"They don't want to talk to me anymore? I don't understand."

"The NTSB said they will continue their interview with you at a later date, and the chief pilot wants you out of Honolulu. He said you're too hot with the press right now, and he wants you to lay low at home. This is for your protection, Kerri."

"Can I at least go back to the hotel to change?"

"No. Sorry. Your flight leaves in forty minutes. We'll head through Flight Operations, walk across the ramp, and go up the outside Jetway stairs. That way you can avoid the press at the airport. I also have some civilian clothes for you at Flight Ops, so you can change."

"Thanks, Camille."

Kerri was grateful Camille was watching out for her, and that the chief pilot was trying to protect her. Maybe some time off at home would be good for her. She was never able to spend as much time as she wanted to with her old dog, Brownie. She also had closets to clean out and movies to catch up on. Who was she kidding? She'd be miserable at home alone.

So many things were out of her control in her life. She couldn't fly, couldn't see Janine, and couldn't fight back against outrageous accusations. She could only try to take care of herself and figure out how to get Janine away from Ryan.

The company put her on a plane to San Francisco, then to Los Angeles, to avoid the press. The crew on the flight to San Francisco was very kind. Out of professional courtesy, no one asked her any questions about the accident. Each of them knew an emergency could happen to one of them, on any given day they flew.

When she finally got home to her quiet, high-rise condo overlooking the ocean, her faithful dog, Brownie, greeted her with the same enthusiasm she always did. Kerri bent down to pet her sweet angel, and then she sat down on the floor with her dog. She held Brownie and ran her fingers through her soft fur as tears ran down her cheeks. Her dog had been with her through several breakups over the years and always gave her unconditional love and acceptance. Kerri was so thankful Brownie was still here with her, not judging her flying skills or her decision-making ability.

She looked out the big windows at the view she adored. Seeing the Pacific Ocean from her balcony always made her feel calm and centered. Today, however, the sea did nothing to calm her restlessness. She felt totally helpless.

But she had to be patient and wait for the NTSB investigation to run its course before she could clear her name and get her pilot's license back. She also had to wait until Janine could message her. Waiting was Kerri's least favorite thing. Suddenly a sharp knock at her door interrupted her thoughts.

A young man stood before her. "Excuse me, but are you Kerri Sullivan?"

"Yes. Who wants to know?"

"You've been served." He handed her an envelope, turned, and quickly walked away.

Kerri closed and locked the door, then opened the white envelope. She read the contents. "Are you fucking kidding me? What's next?"

David Shapiro was suing her for ten million dollars.

A dark cloud descended on her. The walls seemed to be closing in on her, and she had nowhere to run. She couldn't even leave her own home without a pack of reporters following her. The NTSB had taken flying from her, Ryan had taken Janine from her, and now David Shapiro was trying to take her financial security. She couldn't possibly afford a ten-million-dollar judgment against her. Kerri held on to Brownie, her only friend in the world right now.

❖

Janine looked for George Cato in the hotel conference room filled with flight attendants. She hated leaving Molly alone with Ryan, even for a few minutes, but she had to speak to George.

The company emergency-procedures instructors asked the flight attendants about their actions during the evacuation, the ditching, and their time in the life rafts. All the emergency equipment had worked as it was supposed to, with a few notable exceptions. The instructors were stunned when they realized how far Janine's raft had drifted away from the other rafts due to the loss of their sea anchor. By having the sea anchor in place, the other three life rafts had stayed fairly close together near the accident site. Her coworkers and their passengers were in their rafts for only a few hours before a nearby cargo ship picked them up.

When Janine told them about losing their emergency locator transmitter in the storm, the instructors couldn't believe they'd been rescued.

"How in the world did that navy research ship find you?" the lead instructor asked.

"Captain Sullivan showed a young passenger how to use our signal mirror, the navy ship saw it, and then they found us."

The entire room of airline professionals was silent.

"It's a miracle your raft was found, and we're so glad you're all right. We will definitely implement some changes to better secure the sea anchor and the ELT to the rafts, now that we know how easy it is to lose this critical equipment. You all did an outstanding job, and you saved the lives of two hundred and fifty passengers. Thank you for your cooperation. We have counselors available if anyone needs to talk."

Janine spotted George moving toward the exit and hurried over to talk to him.

"Janine, honey, I'm so happy to see you!" George put his arms around her neck and pulled her into a big hug.

"I need to talk to you. I need help." She maneuvered him over to a private corner.

"What is it, darling?"

"How well do you know Kerri?"

"As well as I know anyone I've ever flown with."

"Good, because we both need your help."

"We? Are you two a thing now?" George smiled.

Janine paused but then smiled. "Yes, we are."

"I'm so happy for you." George grabbed her shoulders and pulled her into another hug.

"I need to see her, but my husband is very controlling, and I need to get away from him for a while. Can you help us out?"

"Maybe. When are you due for recurrent training?"

"Next month."

"Good. I'll call Dusty, in Crew Scheduling, and ask her to move up your training class. We can ask for the late class start time in San Francisco, so you have to spend the night to finish day two. Kerri could fly up to SF and meet you at the crew layover hotel."

"That sounds perfect."

Light entered Janine's heart at the thought of being with Kerri again.

"What are you going to do about your husband?" George reached for her hand.

"I'm not sure. I still have to figure that out. Thank you."

Janine bent down to kiss his cheek. By the time she got back to the hotel room, her cell phone was ringing. Ryan answered it.

"Who is this, please?"

He listened a few seconds, then handed the phone to Janine. "It's the Crew Desk."

"Hello, this is Janine. Just a second, let me get a pen. Recurrent training in SFO, start time three p.m., day after tomorrow. Got it. Thank you, Dusty."

"What's this about training? You're supposed to be off duty until the investigation is done." Ryan looked irritated.

"The Crew Desk said I will expire on recurrent training soon, so I have to go to San Francisco on Monday, for two days."

"Well, Molly and I will just go to San Francisco with you. Maybe I'll take her to the zoo while you're in class."

"No, Ryan. She needs to get back to school and to her physical therapy. She's already missed several days. You could take her to school and meet her teacher. Or Rosa can take her and pick her up."

Janine knew Ryan wasn't comfortable being around Molly by himself for too long. She gave him an easy out.

"Well, if you're sure this Rosa is a reliable person, it's all right with me if she takes Molly to school."

"Thank you, Ryan. I'll only be gone two days."

A tingle ran down Janine's spine. She would see Kerri soon, and they would have a whole night together. She was breathless.

❖

Monday, May 12

Kerri was enjoying herself for the first time in a long time. Driving north on the Pacific Coast Highway, with the top down on her blue convertible, she was listening to some of her favorite women singers, feeling the wind in her hair. She glanced at her watch—two hours to go. Kerri cranked up the tunes for the rest of her drive to San Francisco. She would arrive at the layover hotel an hour before Janine finished training, which would give her plenty of time to clean herself up and set the mood in the hotel room.

Kerri had been beyond happy when George Cato had called her last night to tell her about the rendezvous plan with Janine.

She'd been struggling at being forced to hide out in her own home. Alternating between sadness and anger, she was going stir-crazy. A drive up the beautiful California coast to see Janine was just what she needed.

Kerri didn't want to jinx anything, but she couldn't stop herself from listening to some mushy, romantic music. She realized she was getting her hopes up, with a possibility they'd get crushed, but this was different. This wasn't just another fling with a beautiful, hot woman. This felt like a beginning.

Kerri wasn't sure what form this beginning would take, but she sensed it to be very special. Her feelings for Janine had only grown stronger, in spite of everything they'd endured. Maybe she desired Janine so intensely because they'd almost died together, but then she remembered their time in the skipper's cabin.

She thought of the first time she'd touched Janine's velvety skin, when she caressed Janine's luscious breasts, when she pressed her thigh into Janine's center—those sensations were real and powerful. She had to have more.

Kerri stood up at the sound of the key in the room lock, holding her breath.

Janine looked so beautiful when she walked into the room. She stopped, they looked at each other a moment, and then Kerri closed the distance between them and wrapped her arms around Janine. Their lips met, and they kissed like they'd been lovers separated for years.

"Wait. Let me catch my breath." Janine stepped back and held Kerri's face in her palms.

"You're so beautiful, Kerri. I've missed you so much."

Janine leaned in and pressed her lips to Kerri's with long, languid kisses. Her tongue made slow lines across Kerri's lower lip. She pulled Janine closer to her and pressed her breasts into Janine's full mounds. Janine started gyrating her hips against Kerri.

"Let's lie down. Can I help you out of your dress?"

Janine chuckled. "Why, yes, Captain. You certainly can."

They quickly undressed, Kerri hung up Janine's uniform, and then she turned down the bed for them. They pressed their naked bodies together, wrapping their arms and legs around each other. She shuddered with Janine's satin skin and firm body pressed against hers. They exchanged slow, deep kisses while they explored the wonders of each other. Kerri kissed her and slid her tongue into Janine's hot mouth, arousal spreading throughout her. The desire to make love with Janine was overwhelming, but did Janine really want this also?

"I know what you're thinking. You're afraid Ryan has damaged me, and you're worried about me. I love that you care. I'm all right, and I really want to make love with you."

Kerri had no more worries. They spent the rest of the night touching and tasting every square inch of each other. Kerri couldn't keep her hands off Janine's full breasts. They were so responsive, and Kerri loved the sound Janine made when she sucked her nipples. Their fears and hesitations faded into the night, as the last light of day changed from blue, to lavender, to dark purple. Nothing in the world existed but this space, with the two of them melding into one body, one heart, making their love become tangible and real. They felt safe with each other and brought each other to ecstasy over and over.

"You're the most amazing lover I've ever had," Janine whispered, her head next to Kerri's on the pillow.

A slow wave rolled over her. It wasn't scary but was light and magical. A thought, with perfect clarity, came into her mind. *I love you.*

Part of her feared it was too soon to say this, but a much bigger part of her was filled with joy. It had been so long since she felt anything real for another woman, anything beyond superficial attraction. She had enormous respect for Janine. Kerri admired her, desired her, and could see them having a future life together.

Janine rolled onto her side and snuggled her back against Kerri's front.

"What are you thinking?"

Kerri hesitated, but the wave of emotion was too much for her. She had to tell Janine the truth, or she might combust.

"I love you."

Janine froze. Then she rolled over slowly to face Kerri. "Really?"

"Yes. I really love you, Janine. I know I'm getting way ahead of myself, but I had to tell you, or I would burst."

Janine gently kissed Kerri's lips. "I love you too."

CHAPTER TWENTY

Tuesday, May 13

Janine woke up early, the soft light of morning peeking through the hotel window. She heard Kerri's steady breathing and relished the sensation of being pressed against her body. Kerri snorted, put her arm across Janine's waist, and pulled Janine closer to her. Kerri's hand on her belly gave Janine shivers of pleasure, as she remembered their lovemaking last night. She wanted more.

Janine had been with a few people before she met Ryan. She'd always enjoyed herself in bed, but no one ever rocked her world like Kerri had. More than anything, Janine was attracted to Kerri's kind heart.

Kerri rarely showed this side of herself, because she always had to be the calm leader at work, the fearless Captain Sullivan. Alone together, Janine saw how tender Kerri was to her during their lovemaking. She was an unhurried, considerate lover, who clearly enjoyed every moment, from the softest caresses to giving Janine powerful, mind-blowing orgasms. She had never felt so connected, both physically and spiritually, to another person. She was living in a beautiful dream.

Janine glanced at the clock radio. She had one hour before she had to get ready for class, and they had some important decisions to make. Kerri's hand moved from her belly to the underside of her breast and started squeezing Janine's fullness. She needed to discuss things with Kerri, but for now, only Kerri's hot, powerful body was on her mind. She couldn't stop herself from writhing against Kerri's lap. Putting her hand on top of Kerri's, she guided it to where she needed it most and whispered, "Harder."

"Ummm," Kerri replied. Then she moved her thigh between Janine's legs and pressed into her center. Janine was very aroused as she rolled onto her stomach and spread her legs wide for Kerri. Janine hungered for her again. She wanted Kerri's weight on her body, Kerri's fingers inside her, and she didn't hold back expressing her desire. She closed her eyes and let Kerri send her over a cliff with wave after wave of ecstasy until she was spent again.

"I don't want to ever leave this room." Kerri nuzzled her face into Janine's silky blond hair.

Janine sighed. "Neither do I, but we have to talk about some things before I leave."

Kerri climbed out of bed and made them two cups of coffee. "Here you go, babe."

Janine liked hearing Kerri call her "babe." "Thank you. We have to figure out a plan."

"I agree. What do you want to do?"

"I want you to live with Molly and me, somewhere far away from Ryan."

"How are we going to do that, if you're still married to him? I thought you said he was your ex-husband. What do you want to do about him?"

Janine was quiet, then reached over to hold Kerri's hand. "I'm sorry I didn't tell you the full story. In my mind, he is an ex, even though we're still legally married."

"Why don't you just divorce him?"

"Because I signed a prenup giving him control of everything. I was temporarily out of my mind because of my pregnancy hormones. I had to drop out of college, my parents didn't want anything to do with me, and I had no money and no choices. It was the only way I could take care of Molly."

Kerri squeezed her hand. "I'm so sorry. But how can we be free together with you still married to him? Why don't you hire an attorney and be done with him?"

Janine hesitated. She wanted to be truthful to Kerri, but her fear held her back. If Kerri knew the full truth about how sick and twisted her relationship with Ryan was, she wouldn't want anything to do with her.

Kerri held both her hands and looked deep into her eyes.

Janine gazed back at the beautiful brown eyes filled with compassion and love. She trusted Kerri with her life, so maybe she could trust Kerri with her awful past.

She grabbed a box of tissues, leaned back against the headboard, and let her mind unlock the dungeon of secrets about Ryan Jackson.

Janine let out a big sigh. "He hid his true self from me until after Molly was born. By the time I fully understood the depths of his depravity, it was too late. He had control over all my finances and every aspect of my life."

Janine struggled to get the words out. As she recounted her life with Ryan, the shame and humiliation returned like it was yesterday. She tried to suppress her memories, but she wanted Kerri to know her full story. She held Kerri's hand, took a deep breath, and continued.

"He drugged me. I was never sure what it was, but I think it was some type of roofie. I'd wake up the next morning covered with bruises and no memory of how I got them. That went on for quite a while, and then he started including other people in his sick games."

"Why didn't you get away from him?"

"I tried, Kerri. So many times. I was powerless. Whenever I started to leave, he would throw that prenup in my face. In the agreement I signed, if I ever divorced him, Ryan would have full custody of Molly. I decided to take whatever he did to me in order to protect Molly."

Tears rolled down her face. All the awful feelings flooded over her again as if it were yesterday.

"Then there was that video."

"What video?"

"He has a video of me." She could barely choke out the words. "It shows me having sex with all these different men, one after another, when I was under the influence of his drugs."

"Oh, my God, Janine." Kerri held her hand tighter.

"Whenever I told him I wanted out, he would threaten to release that video. Then one day, he went too far, and I ended up in the emergency room. Apparently, he just dumped me off in front of the ER and drove away. I don't remember much, but I do recall seeing the police at the hospital. Then Ryan's parents showed up. They pretended to care about me, but they were really there to make sure there would be no official reports. They also reminded me of the prenup. I felt absolutely trapped."

Kerri held Janine. With Kerri's arms around her, the tears came out of her in wave after wave of regret.

"After all that, how did you get away from him?"

"I tolerated his abuse because I thought I was saving Molly from him. Then one day, when she was two years old, I heard Ryan giving Molly a bath, and he was talking to her in his creepy sex voice. I knew, without any doubt, that she would be next. I had to get her away from him before he hurt her. That's when I put together my plan. I found a guy who could help me get a new identity. Then I waited until Ryan left to go on one of his overseas sex trips and raided his safe, took fifty grand in cash, and we escaped. I've been looking over my shoulder ever since, in dread of Ryan finding us. When he saw my picture on TV, he found Molly. Seeing him hold Molly when we got off that navy ship was the worst day of my life."

"Does Ryan know about you and me?"

"No. If he did, he'd have one of his thugs threaten you to stay away from me."

Kerri didn't say anything. She wrapped her arms around Janine and held her. "So what do we do about him?"

"Kerri, I have to know something first. After all the awful stuff I just told you, you must think I'm a weak, helpless person. Why would you want to be with me?"

"Oh, Janine, how can you ask me that? A master manipulator tricked you. I'm guessing he's done this to many other women for a long time. He slipped up when he got you pregnant, and his wealthy parents forced him to marry you to save their reputation."

Kerri turned and held Janine's face with both hands.

"Janine, you are not responsible for Ryan's actions. He is. When you let him hurt you, in order to protect Molly from him, you were proving that you're one of bravest women I've ever met. You showed me how strong you were when we were in that raft. You kept doing your job, you took care of our passengers, and you gave them encouragement and hope to hang on. I have nothing but respect, admiration, and love for you."

Kerri pulled her close and gently kissed her tear-stained face.

"I think we just have to bide our time until the NTSB investigation ends. I'm stuck until then. I'm worried they're going to blame me for the accident and I'll never fly again." She choked up as she said those last words.

"But it wasn't your fault, Kerri. I was with you on the flight deck when we lost cabin pressure, and you didn't do anything wrong."

"That doesn't matter. Whenever a plane crashes, the pilots are always blamed first. They have to find evidence to prove what the cause was, and they haven't found anything, so far. I can't go anywhere with you and Molly until this mess is over."

"I understand. I have to get ready for class."

Janine quickly styled her hair, put on her makeup and uniform dress, and bent down and kissed Kerri on the cheek.

"I have to go. I will do whatever I have to do to protect Molly. I hope you can find a way to be with us."

Janine zipped her roller-board suitcase closed, walked to the door, and turned to Kerri. "I love you."

"I love you too."

As Janine walked down the hotel hallway, sadness descended on her. After a beautiful night of lovemaking with Kerri, she had no idea when they could see each other again. She didn't know if Kerri would be willing to run away from Ryan to live in a foreign country with her. She wasn't even sure Kerri wanted to live with a special-needs child. For now, she would have to play along with Ryan to keep Molly safe. Maybe the only solution was one she'd thought about many times.

I'm going to have to kill him to be free.

CHAPTER TWENTY-ONE

The hotel room felt lonely after Janine left. The scent of her perfume lingered in the air, and Kerri longed to hold her again. She quickly showered and dressed, then drove back to Los Angeles. The drive down the Pacific Coast was beautiful, but Kerri couldn't enjoy it because she was worried about Janine and Molly. She hadn't even met Molly, but she cared about her and wanted to take care of her because Janine loved her so much. Kerri was afraid for their safety with Ryan. The jangling of her phone interrupted her thoughts.

"Is this Captain Sullivan?"

"Yes, it is."

"This is the NTSB secretary, and I'm calling to tell you to report tomorrow morning at nine a.m. to our Los Angeles office for the hearing. I'm sending you the information via email."

Kerri was surprised this was happening so soon. "Have they found the airplane and the flight recorders?"

"I'm not allowed to talk about that subject. Just make sure you're at the hearing tomorrow. Good-bye."

Fear gnawed at her stomach.

❖

Wednesday, May 14

Kerri arrived at the NTSB office five minutes before nine and was surrounded by a sea of reporters at the building's entrance. Then she saw her friend Camille waiting for her. "I'm so glad to see you. Have they told you anything?"

"No. I thought you might've heard something. I'm glad you wore your uniform. You look great, Kerri."

"Well, I don't feel great. I just want to get this over with."

They went inside a big room packed with people, with cameras everywhere, and sat down at the table facing the raised platform where the NTSB investigators were. Kerri took a seat next to her former first officer.

"Hi, Ray. How're you doing?" Kerri asked.

"I've been better. How're you holding up?"

"I'm okay. I just wish this was done."

"Me too. I wanted to tell you that I'm sorry I couldn't be more helpful at the preliminary hearing in Honolulu. I wish I could remember more of what happened."

"Don't worry about it, Ray. You did the best you could."

The sharp sound of a wooden gavel stopped their conversation.

"This hearing of the National Transportation Safety Board will now come to order."

Oh, great. It's him again.

"I am Robert Ellsworth, vice-chairman of the NTSB, and I'd like to welcome everyone to the accident investigation hearing for the loss of Trans Global flight 401. We will present all the evidence we have acquired so far, then take statements from the crew members involved in this mishap."

Kerri glanced around the room looking for Janine and spotted her sitting in the last row, with Ryan on one side and George Cato on the other. They made eye contact briefly, and Janine gave her a small smile. The fear in her belly dissipated when she saw Janine's beautiful face. Ryan leaned over and said something in her ear that made Janine scowl and lower her head. *Bastard.*

"We will begin the hearing today by summarizing the facts we have so far, keeping in mind that we are still searching for the cockpit voice recorder and the digital flight data recorder. We will then continue with questions of the flight crew members. Please be advised that we expect truthful and complete answers. Evasiveness will not be tolerated."

Kerri felt that last statement was directed at her. She had nothing to hide and had been completely honest with all her answers so far. She listened as panel members presented the details of the flight, up to the moment the emergency began. Then they covered the engine data transmitted just before they lost cabin pressure. They talked at length explaining the engine parameters of the high-bypass turbofan engines. Kerri saw eyes glaze over in the crowd as they went into excruciating detail of how a jet engine works.

Kerri started feeling uncomfortable as the investigators produced charts showing how reliable the Pratt and Whitney engines were, with special attention to the two engines installed on her jet. Both of her engines had been in service for years and had thousands of flight hours with no history of any significant engine malfunctions.

Ellsworth then called on the Boeing 767 chief engineer.

"The Boeing 767 is one of the safest aircraft ever built. It is highly unlikely that an engine would simply disintegrate when operating at a stable cruise altitude."

"Is it possible for the engine to be damaged by operator error, such as abruptly pulling the throttle to idle?" Ellsworth looked at Kerri as he asked the question.

"Yes, it is."

Ellsworth asked the same question of the Pratt and Whitney chief engineer and received the same response. He repeated his line of questions with the Trans Global chief of flight training.

Kerri realized Ellsworth was painting a picture of her as

an incompetent pilot. He was planting seeds of doubt about her actions as the captain of flight 401. She was seething at the implication that she had intentionally damaged her own aircraft, especially since he had no proof she'd done anything wrong. He was setting her up to be the fall guy, and she was helpless to defend herself.

"We will recess until one p.m. Then we will continue with questions for the crew."

Kerri was watching her entire career as a professional pilot unravel in front of her.

❖

Janine left the hearing room with heaviness on her heart for Kerri. She didn't understand all the stuff about jet engine malfunctions, but Kerri would never damage her own plane. She cared too much about her crew and passengers to ever harm any of them.

Janine stood with George and the other flight attendants, who all had somber expressions.

"Can I talk to you for a minute?" It was David Shapiro, their difficult first-class passenger.

"What can we do for you, Mr. Shapiro?" George asked.

"You can join my class-action lawsuit against Captain Kerri Sullivan. Her incompetence almost got all of us killed. We deserve substantial compensation for the horror we all went through because of her."

George Cato stood up to his full height of five feet four inches and stepped into David Shapiro's personal space.

"First of all, none of us knows anything definitive yet as to the cause of this accident. Second, I've flown with Kerri Sullivan for years, and she's the best captain I've ever worked with. I don't believe any of these implications about her intentionally damaging the plane. It makes no sense. So, no, I will not join your lawsuit."

"What about you, Janine? Will you join my class-action suit?"

Janine started to answer, but Ryan interrupted her. "Yes. We want to be part of your lawsuit." He glared at Janine to shut her up.

"But, Ryan, I don't want any part of his lawsuit."

He grabbed Janine by her upper arm, jerked her away from the others, and got very close to her face.

"Don't you ever disagree with me in public. You're too stupid to understand that this lawsuit is good for my campaign, and this will get us sympathy back home. You will join in with that lawsuit and keep your mouth shut, or else."

David Shapiro came up next to them.

"Hey, folks. Could you keep your voices down? People are starting to stare. There's no need for any tension. Just let me know if you're interested."

"We are definitely interested, Mr. Shapiro. Aren't we, Jan?"

Janine kept her head down. She refused to betray Kerri.

"Good. Here's my card. My office will be in touch." David Shapiro walked away quickly.

"Well, it looks like that captain of yours really screwed up," Ryan said.

"You don't know what you're talking about. You weren't there, Ryan. I'm not suing Kerri Sullivan."

"You'll do what you're told." He stomped away, barely containing his rage.

Her desperation to get away from Ryan made Janine want to scream out loud, but now wasn't the time. She had to pretend to cooperate with him for a little while longer.

There was a buzz in the crowd, and someone said, "Let's get back in there. Something's happening."

Janine wished she could sit next to Kerri, just to comfort her. She'd been very stoic so far, but Janine could tell these accusations were getting to her.

❖

"This hearing will come to order," Ellsworth said as he pounded the table with his gavel.

Kerri looked around the room, hoping to see Janine. Then she saw Camille rush up to the microphone.

"Mr. Ellsworth, we've just been advised there is new evidence about this accident."

"Where is it?"

"Right here, sir."

"And who are you?" Ellsworth asked.

"I'm Lieutenant Commander Stacey Gentry, Commander of the US Navy Research Vessel *Sally Ride.* We found Trans Global 401."

A collective gasp rose from the crowd.

Stacey Gentry looked magnificent in her white dress uniform as she strode up to the front of the room. She handed a disc to the audio/visual person, then rolled out a navigation chart on the table in front of Ellsworth and pointed to a marked spot. "We discovered the aircraft at this position on the sea floor."

Kerri saw the reporters scramble out the back of the room to call in this scoop.

"How did you find it? We've been looking for this aircraft for weeks."

"My ship is equipped with the latest underwater mapping technology, and we found it with our ROV—our remotely operated vehicle. Please insert the disc I gave you."

Murmurs arose from the crowd as the video image showed a dark object on a gray background. The dark mass became larger until it was the unmistakable shape of an airplane.

"We had the ROV move all over the target to make sure we identified it correctly. We positively identified it as Trans Global 401."

The bright headlights of the ROV moved across the tail section. Kerri made out the Trans Global logo and the aircraft tail number. She shivered at the sight of her jet lying on the floor of the ocean. It looked intact, with the plane resting on its belly, the left wing tip in the sand, and the right wing banked up, like it was in a slight turn.

Stacey continued narrating what they were seeing. "We had the ROV scan every part of the aircraft exterior. All parts of the plane are intact except for this area." She used a laser pointer to show where the right wing was attached to the body of the plane. Then the ROV followed the leading edge of the right wing to the wing tip, and it stopped at something that didn't look right. It was a small section, just under the leading edge of the wing, with twisted metal sticking out.

"What are we looking at?" Ellsworth asked.

Kerri jumped up from her seat and shouted, "That's the fuel service panel."

"Please sit down, Captain Sullivan. We'll get to you." Ellsworth glared at her.

"Captain Sullivan is correct. This is the access panel for the single-point refueling station located near the midpoint of the right wing. Please look closely as we have the ROV zoom in to get a better look at this."

The entire room was quiet, everyone transfixed as they watched the eerie underwater images of twisted, bent metal.

Kerri couldn't believe what she was seeing. They used this access panel to refuel the jet every day. It was mangled so badly it was almost unrecognizable. "Oh, my God," she said out loud.

"This metal is torn in a way that indicates high pressure from inside it. Look at the small area on the right side of this compartment at that jagged piece of metal, bright blue in color, which shows clearly it was a can of Pepsi. This is the remnant of a bomb. An explosive device was placed inside the fuel service panel."

The room buzzed. The torn metal was open almost like the petals of a flower.

"We then had the ROV capture a sample of the soda can. You can see the robotic arm grasp the remains of it. When it was returned to my ship for analysis, we confirmed it was filled with

C4 explosive. We then had the ROV do a complete inspection of the area around the bomb blast." Stacey paused for a moment and let the picture of the mangled engine sink in. She glanced at Kerri before she continued.

"This image is the right engine. Notice the black line on the side of it. This is where the ten-inch by eight-inch door of the fuel service panel penetrated the engine cowling and caused the engine to disintegrate."

Everyone started talking at this incredible news. Kerri looked for Janine and smiled.

I'm not responsible for this accident. It was a bomb. That fuel guy, with the clean shirt and neat handwriting, he planted the bomb.

"Order, order." Ellsworth pounded his gavel.

Stacey continued. "On further analysis, we found several puncture holes on the underside of the right wing, where the fuel tank is located, and we saw the remains of a cabin window blown inside the aircraft. This discovery confirms that metal shrapnel from the bomb explosion punctured the window from outside, and caused the aircraft to lose cabin pressure."

The remaining reporters scrambled out of the room to call in this new information to the media.

Ellsworth rapped his gavel on the table again. "Order, please."

After the room grew quiet again, he said, "Lieutenant Commander Gentry, this is a very interesting speculation, but we deal with facts, not guesses." His tone was dismissive.

"That's why I brought this with me today, sir. Gunny, please bring in the boxes."

Kerri recognized one of the marines from Stacey's ship as he pushed a cart to the front of the room holding three plastic tubs filled with water.

"This is the digital flight data recorder, the cockpit voice recorder, and the remnants of the explosive device. We were able to retrieve these using our ROV. They should have all the information from the accident."

The room erupted in noise. Ellsworth banged his gavel, but no one was listening to him anymore. Finally, he got everyone calmed down.

"Lieutenant Commander Gentry, thank you for providing this important evidence to the NTSB. We will need to do our own analysis of this information before reaching any conclusions about the cause of this accident. This hearing is adjourned for now, and we will reconvene when our investigators complete their work with the aircraft recorders. You are dismissed."

He banged his gavel one last time.

An enormous weight lifted off Kerri's shoulders. She knew she hadn't made a mistake and caused this accident, and Stacey Gentry had just saved her ass with the proof. She wanted to run to Janine and put her arms around her, but Ryan had his hand on her arm and hurried her out of the room.

Camille hugged Kerri. "Well, you've got friends in high places."

"What do you mean?"

"Not everyone has their own navy research ship find evidence to exonerate them. We got real lucky, Kerri."

"So what happens now?"

"We wait for the NTSB laboratory to analyze the data and voice recorders, and test that bomb remnant. Then they'll reconvene and present their findings. That should take only a few days. It looks like you're off the hook, Kerri."

People had crowded around Kerri to congratulate her when she recognized a familiar voice behind her.

"Captain Sullivan, can I talk to you?"

Kerri was surprised to see David Shapiro standing before her with his hand outstretched.

"Mr. Shapiro, what can I do for you?"

"I need to apologize. I thought you were to blame for the

accident. I can't believe a bomb in a soda can could cause that much damage to the plane. I was wrong to accuse you. I'm sorry."

Kerri decided to be gracious to this man who had caused her such grief. She extended her hand to him.

"I'm dropping my lawsuit, of course, but can I do anything to make up for my actions?" He sounded sincere.

"Mr. Shapiro, I accept your apology. But you know what? You could use your skills as an attorney to help people instead of hurt them."

Kerri turned from him to look around the room, hoping to see Janine. She caught a glimpse of Janine's golden hair. She was being shuttled out of the room, with Ryan's hand on the back of her neck. She clenched her jaw. *I have to get her away from him.*

CHAPTER TWENTY-TWO

Kerri walked into her dark, quiet home, leaned against the closed door, and inhaled deeply of the scent of the ocean. Calmness washed over her like a warm wave. She cherished the sound of Brownie's toenails tap-tapping across the wood floor to greet her.

She bent down to hold her old dog in a long hug. Brownie had seen her through some difficult times, but none as hard as the last few weeks.

"How about I cook us a nice steak on the grill tonight? I know you like it."

Brownie danced at the sound of her favorite word.

The ring of Kerri's phone interrupted their joy. She decided to take a chance and answer the unknown number.

"This is Stacey. You home? I need to change out of my uniform."

"Uh, okay, come on up. I'm in number—"

"I know the number."

Two minutes later, a sharp knock sounded at the door.

"Come on in."

"Nice place, Kerri. Great view of the water. I don't suppose you have anything to drink?"

"How about some Crown Royal?"

"Great. Two fingers, over ice. Mind if I change?"

"Go right ahead." Kerri was perplexed and feeling a little awkward. *Why is she here? And what does she want?*

When she returned to the living room with the drinks, Stacey was sitting in her recliner, wearing cut-off jean shorts and a snug tank top with no bra.

"Thanks for the drink. You must be wondering why I'm here."

"I was kind of curious."

"Before you hear anything from the news media, or even the US Navy, I wanted to tell you the truth about how I found your plane."

Kerri took a big gulp of her drink. "I'm listening."

"I knew you were being set up to take the fall, and I couldn't let that happen again."

"What do you mean, again?"

"There have been some incidents where women pilots were blamed for accidents they didn't cause, just because they were females. I saw this happen to a friend of mine, one of the first navy women fighter pilots. She was fairly new to the F-14, and she had the inboard engine blow up in the final turn for a carrier landing, she couldn't eject, and she died in the plane crash. Her male squadron mates released her confidential training records to the press to show she was a weak pilot. She'd busted only one ride in training, but they crucified her before they even started the investigation.

"The same thing was about to happen to you. I had a feeling you didn't do anything wrong with those engines, but we had to prove it by finding the data recorders."

"I can't believe what I'm hearing. Why would anyone want to blame me instead of find out the truth?"

"There's an agenda at work here, just like there has been for all the years women have been making strides in the military. A lot of boys out there still don't want us in their club houses. If they can blame a woman for an airplane crash, it proves their point that women are weak pilots and should stay home."

"That's crap. Why are we still fighting these battles forty years after women have been airline pilots?"

"Here's what I came to tell you, Kerri. You're about the luckiest damn woman I ever met. The latitude and longitude coordinates you gave us in your last transmission were right on, but that area of the Pacific Ocean is very deep. Your aircraft settled on an underwater plateau at a depth of only three thousand feet. The sea floor around this plateau is over two miles deep. We would have never found your plane."

"Wow. What are the chances of that?"

"Your 767 stayed intact after a bomb blast and landed, like an angel, on the head of a pin. I filmed all of it, but the navy has it, and now that it's an intentional terrorist bombing, we have to turn everything over to the CIA. They won't be happy with me that I gave the black boxes to the NTSB before they got to look at them, but it was the only way to make sure this information became public."

"I can't believe you did that for me, Stacey. I don't know what to say. Won't you get into trouble with your commander for changing course to find my plane?"

"Not really. I had the opportunity to field-test some prototype search equipment. Let's just say they were very pleased. This is a copy of all the raw footage we took of your plane. Keep it in a safe place, and only use it in an emergency. By the way, the fuel guy who planted the bomb on your plane is a Saudi national and a known terrorist. He was in the country legally on a student visa. When they picked him up, he had a dozen soda-can bombs at his apartment. He had big plans. Got to go. Thanks for the drink."

"Thank you, Stacey. You saved my career."

"You just keep helping out the next young women who want to fly, and we'll be square."

Kerri was grateful for her new friend. Stacey would be someone she could count on for a long time.

She looked at her phone for the hundredth time, hoping to see a text from Janine. Her worry was escalating. Now that the truth was out about the bomb attack on her jet, Ryan would want to get Janine and Molly back to his family's fortress so he could use her fame to help his political campaign.

"Please, Janine, let me know you're all right." She whispered her prayer to the ocean.

❖

The phone rang, and Ryan snatched it from Janine's hand.

"Janine Case's phone. Who is this, please?" His sickly sweet voice made Janine want to vomit. He put the phone on speaker mode so he could hear every word said.

"This is the Crew Desk, calling for Janine."

"This is Janine. Go ahead."

"The crew bus will pick you up at seven thirty tomorrow morning. The NTSB just informed us they have completed their investigation, and the final results will be announced at their downtown office. Please wear your uniform."

"Thank you."

Ryan shut off her phone. "Good. The sooner we get through this investigation, the sooner we can get home and get busy with my campaign. How about if I give you a gift of some nice, big breast implants to celebrate?"

Tomorrow. That will be my chance to get away from him. Kerri will be there, and I'll make my break for freedom.

❖

Thursday, May 15

The next morning, Janine felt safe standing next to George Cato and the rest of their crew, just outside the hearing room. She kept scanning the crowd for Kerri's face. The doors opened and they all filed in. Kerri was already sitting at the front table with Ray.

"Please take your seats, ladies and gentlemen. This won't take too long." Ellsworth didn't even pound his gavel on the desk and scowled less than he had the previous days.

"I want to thank Lieutenant Commander Gentry, and the crew of the USS *Sally Ride,* for finding the aircraft, and for retrieving the black boxes. This investigation would have been much more difficult without your assistance. I also want to thank the representatives from Boeing, Pratt and Whitney, and Trans Global for your cooperation. Our analysis of the cockpit voice recorder, the digital flight data recorder, and all other transmitted data is complete."

A small murmur ran through the crowd. Janine couldn't take her eyes off Kerri, sitting at the table in front with Ray. She had a calm, expressionless appearance. She was trying to look professional, but Janine knew she was cheering inside.

They had been through so much trauma in the last two weeks. From almost getting blown to bits from a bomb, to landing on the water, then the emergency evacuation, and finally, surviving on a raft for two days. For Janine, the most traumatic part was finding Ryan with her daughter.

Janine didn't have much in the way of an escape plan. She'd briefly considered hiring a hit man to take out Ryan, but that wasn't who she was. She had been afraid of Ryan for years, but seeing her airplane on the bottom of the ocean yesterday had changed everything for her.

When Janine had seen the camera move over the hull of the underwater airplane, her overpowering feeling was, "That was almost me."

When it was clear just how close they'd all come to being killed by a bomb, two thoughts broke through her consciousness. First, she had survived this situation for a reason. Whatever that was, her number wasn't up yet. Maybe it was to take care of Molly, or maybe it was to be with Kerri. Regardless of the reason, she refused to waste one more minute of her life running away from Ryan. That led to her second thought. After what she'd been through, she was no longer consumed with fear—of Ryan, or of anyone.

Janine would not run and hide. She would stand up to him and demand a divorce. She would deal with whatever consequences her prenup might cause, and she would fight for Molly. With Kerri by her side, they could get through anything. Janine also understood the value of publicity, and Ryan would avoid a scene.

Janine listened to Ellsworth as he continued with the NTSB findings.

"We have positively confirmed that a compact explosive device was planted in the fuel service area of the leading edge on the right wing. This device exploded in mid-flight, causing severe damage to the right engine, an emergency decompression of the cabin, and the subsequent loss of fuel from shrapnel punctures to both wing fuel tanks. In addition, our airframe structural engineers reviewed the damage footage to the right wing. They determined the bomb caused severe damage to the wing spars and surrounding support structures. This damage made the outboard half of the right wing almost separate from the aircraft. If Captain Sullivan had delayed landing the 767 on the water, the wing would have broken off the aircraft, making the airplane uncontrollable, and all passengers and crew would have perished."

A hush moved over the crowd.

"It is our conclusion that Captain Sullivan made the correct assessment of the severity of this emergency, that she made a timely decision to ditch the airplane, and that she did an outstanding job of landing a badly damaged aircraft on the water. In addition, the flight attendant crew successfully evacuated all passengers off the aircraft, got them into the slide rafts, and kept their passengers safe while they awaited rescue."

Cheers rose from the entire room.

"Using the data from the flight recorders and the ROV video, we recreated this scenario in the 767 flight simulator. Out of twenty attempts to complete a water landing of this damaged aircraft, using very experienced 767 pilots, only one crew was able to successfully land the aircraft. Captain Sullivan is to be commended for her exceptional flying skills. All two hundred and fifty passengers owe their lives to the pilots and flight attendants of flight 401. This concludes the final report of the NTSB of this Boeing 767 aircraft mishap. Well done, everyone."

Janine and George hugged each other and all the other flight attendants. They were all smiling with relief. Janine had to get to Kerri. She needed to feel this amazing woman in her arms. As she started to get up from her seat, two large men in black suits approached them.

"Mr. Ryan Jackson?" they asked.

Ryan smiled at being recognized. "Yes, I am."

"Please come with us now." They pulled him out of his seat, lifting him by both his upper arms, and escorted him quickly from the big room.

"Don't go anywhere, Jan. I'll be right back." Ryan glared at her as he was being led from the room.

Janine ignored him and ran to the front of the room to be with Kerri.

❖

Kerri was surprised and elated. She felt like she was lighter than air. This news from the NTSB was the second-best gift she'd ever received. The best one was walking directly toward her. Janine looked magnificent in her blue uniform dress, just like the first time she ever laid eyes on her. Janine gave her a huge smile. Other people crowded around her, congratulating her, but she could see only Janine's beautiful face and stare into her ice-blue eyes. She closed the distance between them, and they held each other tightly.

Kerri felt a small tap at her shoulder. "Are you Captain Kerri?"

A well-dressed older gentleman, with snow-white hair, looked up at her. He reached for her hand and held it with both of his trembling hands.

"Yes, I am."

His voice cracked. "Thank you for saving my George."

Kerri recognized him, even though it had been a long time since she'd seen him.

"Doctor Michael, I'm so glad to see you." She pulled him into a gentle hug.

He couldn't say much more. He just held her hand, but the look of gratitude in his eyes spoke volumes.

George came up to them. "Michael wanted to tell you in person, Kerri. Thank you."

He kissed her on both cheeks. "Come on, Michael. Let's go home."

"Captain Kerri, it's Mel."

Kerri recognized her captain's assistant in the throng of people. "Mel, I'm so happy to see you."

"I want you to meet Mom and Dad."

Mel's mother and father had tears in their eyes. "Thank you for taking care of our girl. We were sick with worry when we got separated from her during the evacuation."

Kerri put her hands on Mel's shoulders. "You should both be very proud of Mel. She's the reason we got rescued. She's a very brave, smart girl."

"I told my mom and dad I want to be a pilot like you when I grow up."

"Good for you. You'll make a great pilot. Look at the U.S. Air Force Academy when you start thinking about college." Kerri gave Mel her business card. "Please stay in touch."

Kerri looked for Janine. She wanted to get away from this crowd and be alone with her.

Then she saw David Shapiro go up to Janine and hand her an envelope.

What the hell is he up to now?

Kerri went over and stood next to Janine, listening to their conversation.

"Janine, this is for you. Please open it when you get home."

"What is it, Mr. Shapiro?"

"It'll be clear when you open it. I'm sorry for my behavior, and I hope this makes up for it. Take care. You're a great lady." He turned and walked into the throng of reporters to make a statement.

"Let's get out of here, Janine."

They slipped out a side door and found a cab to take them to Kerri's home. They held hands while sitting in the back of the vehicle.

"I almost forget to ask, but where's Ryan? Is he with Molly?"

"Frankly, I don't know where he is, and I don't care. I've decided to divorce him and fight that prenup."

"Oh, Janine, I'm so proud of you for standing up to him. I'll help you any way I can."

"I know you will. That's why I think we can beat him, if we stick together."

Kerri looked at Janine's face and tried to memorize it. "I really want to kiss you."

"Me too, Kerri."

"What's in this envelope from David Shapiro?"

They opened it together and pulled out a short stack of legal papers.

"Is this really true?" Janine had a confused look on her face.

"Oh, my God, Janine. I think so. This is a decree of annulment of your marriage to Ryan. This other one is a notarized letter stating the prenuptial agreement you signed is null and void. Open the small letter."

Janine's hands were shaking as she did so.

"There's a note here from the law office of David Shapiro. Listen to this. He says, 'My dear Janine. You will never have to concern yourself with Ryan Jackson again. It turns out that he got into big trouble on a sex trip to Thailand and was more than happy to sign your annulment, void the prenup, and give you full custody of Molly, in order to leave the country and avoid extradition.' I can't believe this."

"Read the rest of it."

"He goes on to say, 'Please forgive me for getting involved in your personal situation, but it was the only way I could say thank you for saving my family's life. I am eternally grateful.' Signed, David."

Janine was very quiet. "Kerri, this is a miracle. We're finally free."

She fell into Kerri's arms and cried tears of relief for the first time.

CHAPTER TWENTY-THREE

Friday, May 31

"Are you ready?"

"Yeah. Let's go!"

Kerri and Janine lifted Molly from her walker into the front right seat of the blue helicopter, buckled her in with the lap belt and shoulder harness, then put the Bose aviation headset over her flame-red hair. She smiled at them, her two front teeth missing, and gave them both an energetic thumbs-up.

They climbed into the back seat of the helicopter, strapped in, and looked out at Hilo airport from the panoramic windows. Their pilot raised the collective lever, and they rose gracefully into the air, gliding over the taxiways, then skimming over the macadamia nut trees to the south. Hawaiian music played over the headsets. It was a perfect day, with the shimmering blue ocean before them, sunshine and puffy clouds above them, and rainbows over waterfalls beneath them.

Kerri was in bliss.

Janine reached over to hold her hand and gave her a dazzling smile. Janine smiled a lot more these days, and she laughed all the time, even though it was more like a guffaw. Kerri adored the sound of Janine and Molly laughing together. They would put each other in stitches over the dumbest jokes. Kerri's goal was to make them laugh out loud every day. So good, so far.

Today was a special treat. Kerri had promised Molly that she could see the Hawaiian goddess of fire, Pele, so they were flying on a tour of the Kilauea volcano. Molly asked nonstop questions of their pilot, but she got very quiet when they first saw the lava field.

It was black, barren terrain, with small clumps of green palm trees spared from the relentless lava. It reminded Kerri of a dark moonscape. Their pilot followed a line of white smoke drifting up from a big crack in the ground. They hovered over it and saw the orange glow of molten rock flowing under the crack.

"These are lava tubes carrying the lava to the sea."

"This is so cool." Molly's excitement was contagious.

Their pilot turned the helicopter, flew down the line of smoke toward the ocean cliff, then put the chopper in a hover. From their safely upwind position, they didn't speak. They all stared at the orange fountains of liquid rock shooting up into the air, then exploding when the hot lava hit the cold ocean. The sight was magnificent and terrifying, both at the same time.

After watching this real fireworks show for several minutes, their pilot said, "Sorry, folks, but we have to head back to Hilo. I hope you enjoyed meeting Pele today."

"I sure did. That was great. Mommy and Kerri, did you see how high that lava went into the air?"

"Yes, Pumpkin, we did. That was amazing." Janine blew Kerri a kiss.

"We got to see new earth being made, right in front of us. That was so awesome."

Molly was right. It was awesome to see new earth created, just as it was to create a new life. A life with Janine and Molly. A new future Kerri had never thought possible. She loved Janine more deeply than she'd ever loved anyone. Janine was authentic, and kind, and brave, and filled with love. Kerri felt so privileged to be loved by her. She looked at Janine's profile.

She was more beautiful today than Kerri had ever seen her. Her golden hair was loose around her face, she looked badass with her Ray-Bans on, and she wore a snug Hawaiian-print T-shirt. Even more beautiful than her appearance was the happiness in the big, bright smile on her gorgeous face.

They'd both learned how life can change in an instant, and you never know how much time you have, so you better make the most of every day.

Their pilot made a beautiful approach and soft landing.

"Can you take a picture of me and my family in front of our helicopter?" Molly handed her phone to the pilot.

"Sure thing." He shut off the engines, and the main rotor slowed down.

Kerri was glad she was wearing sunglasses as she posed with her proud little family. Her happiness was uncontained, and she was so thankful for the gift of love that surrounded her.

Molly scooted between Janine and Kerri, holding both their hands.

"This was the best day, ever."

"It sure was."

About the Author

Julie Tizard is the award-winning author of *The Road to Wings*. She has been a professional pilot for over thirty-five years and was one of earliest women pilots to graduate from U.S. Air Force pilot training. She was an instructor pilot flying the T-37 jet trainer and an aircraft commander flying the KC-10 air refueling tanker. She served in several leadership positions including flight commander, chief of pilot upgrade, chief of flight safety, and squadron commander. Colonel Tizard retired from the Air Force Reserve after twenty-five years of service.

Captain Tizard has been an airline pilot for thirty years and has flown the Boeing 737, 757, and 767, the DC-10, and the Airbus 320. She was an instructor pilot and line check airman on the Boeing 737 fleet. When not talking about flying or attending air shows, she can be found renovating houses, playing a baritone horn in the local LGBT band, and traveling like a normal person. *Flight To The Horizon* is her second novel.

Contact her at JulieATizard@gmail.com or visit her website, www.JulieTizard.com.

Books Available From Bold Strokes Books

Flight to the Horizon by Julie Tizard. Airline captain Kerri Sullivan and flight attendant Janine Case struggle to survive an emergency water landing and overcome dark secrets to give love a chance to fly. (978-1-63555-331-4)

In Helen's Hands by Nanisi Barrett D'Arnuk. As her mistress, Helen pushes Mickey to her sensual limits, delivering the pleasure only a BDSM lifestyle can provide her. (978-1-63555-639-1)

Jamis Bachman, Ghost Hunter by Jen Jensen. In Sage Creek, Utah, a poltergeist stirs to life and past secrets emerge.(978-1-63555-605-6)

Moon Shadow by Suzie Clarke. Add betrayal, season with survival, then serve revenge smokin' hot with a sharp knife. (978-1-63555-584-4)

Spellbound by Jean Copeland and Jackie D. When the supernatural worlds of good and evil face off, love might be what saves them all. (978-1-63555-564-6)

Temptation by Kris Bryant. Can experienced nanny Cassie Miller deny her growing attraction and keep her relationship with her boss professional? Or will they sidestep propriety and give in to temptation? (978-1-63555-508-0)

The Inheritance by Ali Vali. Family ties bring Tucker Delacroix and Willow Vernon together, but they could also tear them, and any chance they have at love, apart. (978-1-63555-303-1)

Thief of the Heart by MJ Williamz. Kit Hanson makes a living seducing rich women in casinos and relieving them of the expensive jewelry most won't even miss. But her streak ends when she meets beautiful FBI agent Savannah Brown. (978-1-63555-572-1)

Face Off by PJ Trebelhorn. Hockey player Savannah Wells rarely spends more than a night with any one woman, but when photographer Madison Scott buys the house next door, she's forced to rethink what she expects out of life. (978-1-63555-480-9)

Hot Ice by Aurora Rey, Elle Spencer, and Erin Zak. Can falling in love melt the hearts of the iciest ice queens? Join Aurora Rey, Elle Spencer, and Erin Zak to find out! A contemporary romance novella collection. (978-1-63555-513-4)

Line of Duty by VK Powell. Dr. Dylan Carlyle's professional and personal life is turned upside down when a tragic event at Fairview Station pits her against ambitious, handsome police officer Finley Masters. ((978-1-63555-486-1)

London Undone by Nan Higgins. London Craft reinvents her life after reading a childhood letter to her future self and, in doing so, finds the love she truly wants. (978-1-63555-562-2)

Lunar Eclipse by Gun Brooke. Moon De Cruz lives alone on an uninhabited planet after being shipwrecked in space. Her life changes forever when Captain Beaux Lestarion's arrival threatens the planet and Moon's freedom. (978-1-63555-460-1)

One Small Step by MA Binfield. In this contemporary romance, Iris and Cam discover the meaning of taking chances and following your heart, even if it means getting hurt. (978-1-63555-596-7)

Shadows of a Dream by Nicole Disney. Rainn has the talent to take her rock band all the way, but falling in love is a powerful distraction, and her new girlfriend's meth addiction might just take them both down. 978-1-63555-598-1)

Someone to Love by Jenny Frame. When Davina Trent is given an unexpected family, can she let nanny Wendy Darling teach her to open her heart to the children and to Wendy? (978-1-63555-468-7)

Uncharted by Robyn Nyx. As Rayne Marcellus and Chase Stinsen track the legendary Golden Trinity, they must learn to put their differences aside and depend on one another to survive. (978-1-63555-325-3)

Where We Are by Annie McDonald. A sensual account of two women who discover a way to walk on the same path together with the help of an Indigenous tale, a Canadian art movement, and the mysterious appearance of dimes. (978-1-63555-581-3)

A Moment in Time by Lisa Moreau. A longstanding family feud separates two women who unexpectedly fall in love at an antique clock shop in a small Louisiana town. (978-1-63555-419-9)

Aspen in Moonlight by Kelly Wacker. When art historian Melissa Warren meets Sula Johansen, director of a local bear conservancy, she discovers that love can come in unexpected and unusual forms. (978-1-63555-470-0)

Back to September by Melissa Brayden. Small bookshop owner Hannah Shepard and famous romance novelist Parker Bristow maneuver the landscape of their two very different worlds to find out if love can win out in the end. (978-1-63555-576-9)

Changing Course by Brey Willows. When the woman of her dreams falls from the sky, intergalactic space captain Jessa Arbelle had better be ready to catch her. (978-1-63555-335-2)

Cost of Honor by Radclyffe. First Daughter Blair Powell and Homeland Security Director Cameron Roberts face adversity when their enemies stop at nothing to prevent President Andrew Powell's reelection. Book 11 in the Honor series. (978-1-63555-582-0)

Fearless by Tina Michele. Determined to overcome her debilitating fear through exposure therapy, Laura Carter all but fails before she's even begun until dolphin trainer Jillian Marshall dedicates herself to helping Laura defeat the nightmares of her past. (978-1-63555-495-3)

Not Dead Enough by J.M. Redmann. In the tenth book of the Micky Knight mystery series, a woman who may or may not be dead drags Micky into a messy con game. (978-1-63555-543-1)

Not Since You by Fiona Riley. When Charlotte boards her honeymoon cruise single and comes face-to-face with Lexi, the high school love she left behind, she questions every decision she has ever made. (978-1-63555-474-8)

Tennessee Whiskey by Donna K. Ford. After losing her job, Dane Foster starts spiraling out of control. She wants to put her life on pause and ask for a redo, a chance for something that matters. Emma Reynolds is that chance. (978-1-63555-556-1)